TEMPLAR DETECTIVE

AND THE

BLACK SCOURGE

A TEMPLAR DETECTIVE THRILLER

Also by J. Robert Kennedy

James Acton Thrillers

Special Agent Dylan Kane Thrillers

Templar Detective Thrillers

Kriminalinspektor Wolfgang Vogel Mysteries

The Colonel's Wife   *Sins of the Child*

Delta Force Unleashed Thrillers

Payback   *Kill Chain*
Infidels   *Forgotten*
The Lazarus Moment   *The Cuban Incident*

Detective Shakespeare Mysteries

Depraved Difference   *Tick Tock*   *The Redeemer*

Zander Varga, Vampire Detective

The Turned

THE TEMPLAR DETECTIVE

AND THE

BLACK SCOURGE

J. ROBERT KENNEDY

UnderMill PRESS

ISBN: 9781990418143

First Edition

For those who didn't make it through.

THE TEMPLAR DETECTIVE

AND THE

BLACK SCOURGE

A TEMPLAR DETECTIVE
THRILLER

"No temptation has overtaken you that is not common to man. God is faithful, and he will not let you be tempted beyond your ability, but with the temptation he will also provide the way of escape, that you may be able to endure it."

Corinthians 10:13

"Be not deceived: Evil companionships corrupt good morals."

Corinthians 15:33

AUTHOR'S NOTE

This is the sixth novel in this series, and for those who have read the others and embraced these characters as so many of you have, please feel free to skip this note, as you will have already read it.

The word "detective" is believed to have originated in the mid-nineteenth century, however, that doesn't mean the concept of someone who investigated crime originated less than two hundred years ago. Crime long predated this era, and those who investigated it as well.

The following historical thriller is intended to be an entertaining read for all, with the concept of a "Templar Detective" a fun play on a modern term. The dialog is intentionally written in such a way that today's audiences can relate, as opposed to how people might have spoken in Medieval France, where, of course, they would have conversed in French and not English, with therefore completely different manners of speaking, and of addressing one another. For consistency, English phrasing is always used, such as Mister instead of Monsieur, for example. This does not mean they will be speaking to each other as rappers and gangsters, but will instead communicate in ways that imply comfort and familiarity, as we would today. If you are expecting, "Thou dost hath offended me, my good sir," then prepareth thyself for disappointment. If, however, you are looking for a fast-paced adventure, with plenty of action, mystery, and humor, then you've come to the right place.

Enjoy.

PREFACE

During the era of the Templar Knights, they amassed a tremendous amount of wealth, much through the fees charged for their letters of credit that allowed the safe transfer of assets from Europe to the Holy Land and back, and for the safe transport of goods, either through heavily guarded caravans, or through their fleets of ships.

These routes spread across Europe, including modern-day Eastern Europe, as well as the Middle East, allowing trade to flourish. Foodstuffs, silks, spices, and more were brought from around the known world and into the noble houses of Europe, enriching the lives of the few who could afford such luxuries.

Yet not everything transported was so innocent, and sometimes those without the best of intentions took advantage.

Sometimes with deadly consequences.

THE BLACK SCOURGE

Paris, Kingdom of France
AD 1298

Jacques Chapon's heart pounded with excitement and fear as he neared his final destination. What he was doing was wrong. It was a betrayal of his wife and family, yet the cravings had to be satisfied. It was nighttime in the slums of Paris in which he ran a bakery with his wife. The business permitted a lifestyle better than most, though it was still meager by the standards of the nobility that ruled them. His vocation allowed him to keep his family warm and fed, all a man could really be expected to do. Yet here he was, rushing through the dark streets of the only city he had ever known, with his wife sleeping peacefully in their bed, under the assumption he lay beside her. It broke his heart every time he slipped out of the house in what was now a nightly habit, something he couldn't manage to break.

He spotted the clothing shop ahead and all his troubles were forgotten as a smile spread, the sweet relief from the pain now gripping him soon at hand. He glanced over both shoulders, making certain he was alone, then ducked into the alleyway beside the shop. He approached the door, again checking to see if anyone was watching, then knocked as instructed to do.

Three raps, then one, then two.

A judas hole in the door slid open, a dim glow from inside revealing a set of eyes he now recognized before it closed. The door was opened and the man guarding it smiled broadly as he stepped aside to let Chapon enter.

"Good evening, Mr. Chapon, it's good to see you again."

"Thank you, you as well."

The man held out a hand and Chapon pressed several coins into it. The hand closed, gripping them tightly, the other indicating the stairs descending to his right.

"Please enjoy yourself."

Chapon smiled. "Thank you." He rushed down the stairs and scanned the surroundings. He was one of the first here this evening, so had the pick of spots in which to partake, except for the reserved ones in the corners, saved for the wealthy clientele who also frequented the location.

A boy rushed down a set of stairs on the opposite side of the basement from those Chapon had descended, then sprinted up to the guard.

"He was followed, sir." The guard at the door looked down the stairs at where the boy was pointing, and Chapon's jaw dropped as he shook his head.

"No, I wasn't! I'm sure I wasn't! I was careful like you told me to be."

The boy shook his head. "He was followed all the way from the bakery. I watched him like you told me to."

"Who followed him?"

The boy shrugged. "I don't know, but he's just around the corner from the alleyway. He's watching the door now."

The guard came down the stairs and jabbed a finger at Chapon. "Don't you dare go anywhere."

A wave of terror flowed through Chapon's body as his strength fled him, and he clamped down tight to prevent himself from soiling his pants. The guard left through the other set of stairs, and the young boy grinned at Chapon.

"You're in trouble now, mister."

"But I didn't know. I didn't see anybody."

A few moments later, the guard returned with someone over his shoulder. He walked into another room off to the side and beckoned Chapon to follow him. Chapon complied and stepped through the door into a room he had never been in before. Whoever it was slung over the man's shoulder was dropped into a chair, and Chapon gasped at who it was.

It was a young man he had known for years, the son of parents that he had considered more than mere customers for almost twenty years. It was a young man who shouldn't be here, who wouldn't be here if it weren't for him.

For Chapon knew exactly why the young man was here, and exactly who had sent him.

Simone Thibault, the woman to whom he owed far too much money, and whose bookkeeper now sat unconscious in front of him, blood trickling from a wound to his forehead.

Thomas Durant.

5

De Rancourt Family Farm
Crécy-la-Chapelle, Kingdom of France
Two days earlier

"Are you happy?"

Thomas Durant's eyebrows shot up at Isabelle Leblanc's question. Though perhaps he shouldn't have been surprised. He had been staring out the window most of the afternoon, his entire body aching, Sir Marcus de Rancourt having given him permission to rest for the remainder of the day after wrenching his shoulder shoveling shit.

So much shit!

He couldn't believe how much shit these animals produced. It was truly staggering. He would no sooner have the barn cleared out and the animals fed, then he'd have to clean it again. It was a never-ending labor about which the two squires, David and Jeremy, delighted in teasing him.

And he hated it.

He truly did.

He had grown up in Paris, the son of a man who used his mind to earn a living. Yes, that brilliant mind had been used for nefarious purposes, yet it was a mind with which he had also been blessed. He had an aptitude for numbers, for math, for reading and writing.

And he was slight—skin and bones, as Lady Joanne had described him—with muscles in name only. Despite toiling for weeks, he still considered himself feeble, though he was improving.

He simply detested the work.

He despised the stink and how it made him reek like one of the beasts he cleaned up after. He wasn't meant for this type of life, and no matter how much he told himself things would get better, he kept thinking of how life had been in Paris working for Mrs. Thibault, using his mind instead of his hands, ending a day of work smelling the same as when it had begun, and with enough money in his pocket to buy a good meal on his walk home.

And it was a home he had grown up in, the only home he knew, where both his mother and father had died. It was all he had to remember them by, and he was being asked to abandon it.

All for the love of the woman who now stared at him, her eyes imploring him to answer.

"Well?"

He sighed. "I fear you won't like the answer."

Her shoulders slumped and her eyes welled with tears. "I knew it."

He reached out for her hand, but she withdrew from him, stepping to the other side of the small farmhouse Sir Marcus had ceded to Lady Joanne and her chambermaid, now friend, Beatrice, when they had sought refuge here last year. "Would you have me lie to you?"

She frowned. "I suppose not, though it might have been easier to hear."

He chuckled, taking a seat at the small kitchen table, gesturing for her to take one as well. She did, though at the far end from him. "I'm just not a farmer. I've never worked this hard in my life for so little reward. In Paris, I had a great job—"

7

"Working for a thief!"

He felt oddly defensive of the woman who had given him a job. Simone Thibault was no saint, of that, there could be no doubt, though none here knew her as he did. She was a complicated woman, a woman who had inherited her husband's lending business years ago after he died. She had been an active and willing participant in his endeavors, so she couldn't plead innocence in that regard, as she had been the brains, and her husband the brawn.

Enzo was now the brawn.

And how so. The man was a beast, easily a head taller than the tallest of men, and twice as wide. He was muscle and bone and anger, yet the most loyal of souls if you were on his good side.

And Thomas was.

At least he hoped he was, having offered Enzo the use of his vacant home while he decided what to do with his life. It had served two purposes—Enzo needed a place to stay as his had burned to the ground a few days before he had left, and it wasn't wise to leave a premises unoccupied for too long in the slums of Paris where he lived.

He regarded the love of his life, the only woman he had ever loved, the only woman he had ever kissed—except for the neighborhood tart when he was a child. "She's not a thief."

"How can you defend such a vile creature?"

"She lends money to those in need."

"And breaks their knees if they don't pay!"

He frowned. "*She* doesn't. Enzo does."

Isabelle leaped from her chair. "I fail to see the difference!"

He extended a hand, urging her to calm down. "The difference is that she helps people in her own way, those who are desperate and have nowhere else to turn. Those that pay her on time are never inconvenienced, and she makes a profit, which allows her to lend to more people."

She stared at him, her eyes wide. "I cannot believe what I'm hearing. You truly have been taken in by this woman, haven't you?"

He frowned. "If you had told me a year ago I would be saying these things, I would have declared you a fool. Yet I didn't know then what I now know, and all isn't as black and white as one would think. I've seen the loans, I keep the books. I know how many people borrow money and pay it back on time. I've seen the lives saved with my own eyes, the shops, the bakers, the butchers. People run into hard times, and she is there to help them when no one else will. Do you think the nobility, the only other people with money, will lend it to wretches like us? Never. You haven't seen the poverty. You haven't seen the desperation when parents can't feed their children because of a minor setback. You live here in this tiny village with the same people you've always known, who are always there to help each other in times of need, because you are all friends and family. You always have food because you live on farms. You don't pay rent to landlords who couldn't care less whether it was you or some other cretin that rented from them. Life here is simpler, easier."

"Then why do you hate it so?"

"Because it's not the life for me!"

Tears rolled down her cheeks at the admission, and

9

she dropped into her chair. "Then how can we ever have a future?"

His chest ached at her words, for he could see no possible way if it meant living here. He stared at her, hope in his eyes. "Would you consider living with me in Paris when we marry?"

Her face brightened and she sat up straight. "Marry?"

His cheeks flushed. "I…I'm sorry, I shouldn't have said that, though, umm, would you consider it?"

Her shoulders slumped. "I fear I'd be as equally unhappy there as you are here." She sighed heavily. "If only there were a way for us to live in both places."

His eyes widened at the thought. "What if there were?"

She stared at him. "Huh?"

"What if there were?" He leaned forward, excited. "Sir Marcus and the others only really need me during growing season. What if we lived in Paris during the winter and I worked for Mrs. Thibault, and during the summer we lived here? I make enough with her that I could easily afford it. It would be the best of both worlds, would it not?"

Her eyes were wide with excitement. "Do you think it could work? I mean, do you think she'd agree to you only working half the year?"

He smiled. "There's only one way to find out."

10

De Rancourt Family Farm
Crécy-la-Chapelle, Kingdom of France

"I can't wait for this infernal winter to be over with."

Templar Knight Sir Marcus de Rancourt glanced at his sergeant, Simon Chastain. "You do realize that the end of winter means planting season, then a summer of backbreaking work."

"Backbreaking work never bothered me, but winters always did. I've been away too long. I'm no longer accustomed to them."

"Myself as well, my friend, though hopefully over the coming years, we'll learn to embrace them as the good people here have."

Simon's eyebrows shot up. "You actually found somebody who embraces winter?"

Marcus chuckled. "The children certainly have."

"Do I look like a child to you?"

"I suppose not."

His youngest of two squires, Jeremy, piped in. "I love the winter. It means you get to warm up by the fire. In the Holy Land, you had no choice in the matter. You were always warming up by the fire of the sun. The only opportunity you ever had to feel the cold was if you were in the desert at night, and then that wasn't a choice either." He frowned. "There are no choices in the Holy Land."

Simon rolled his eyes. "Like you said, only children embrace the winter."

Marcus' other squire, David, punched his friend,

laughing. "Sometimes he does seem to be but a child."

"I'm the same age as you!"

"How could you possibly know? I don't even know what year I was born."

Jeremy shrugged. "Well, almost the same. Hey, wait a moment. Maybe I'm older than you."

"Well, you certainly don't act it, and judging by the amount of hair on your balls, there's no way you're older than me. You've barely hit puberty."

"I'm at least thirty."

"Some people are late bloomers."

Jeremy punched David back. "You're a bastard sometimes, you know that?"

"I am indeed, and I'm not going to change for you."

"Well, at least I'm no longer the youngest here. Thomas is definitely at least ten years my junior, if not fifteen."

"Yes, but I don't think we can count on him," said Marcus.

"Why not? He seems the reliable sort."

"It's not his reliability that I question, it's his happiness. I'm quite certain he's miserable here. He hasn't taken to farm work like I had hoped he would."

"Well, that's because he's done nothing but shovel shit the entire time," said David.

Jeremy grinned. "Saving me from the horrid task. Besides, why—oh no! If he leaves—"

"Exactly. You'll be shoveling shit until the end of time. It suits you, though."

Jeremy growled. "Sometimes I wish I'd never met you."

"Trust me. The feeling's mutual." David turned to

Marcus. "You really think he's unhappy enough that he would leave?"

"Frankly, I'm surprised he's lasted this long. I think the only reason he's here is because Mrs. Thibault hasn't sent a message for him to return yet. Actually, it surprises me she hasn't. Things must be far worse there than she thought it would become."

"Well, an imbalance was created with the massacre of Pequin and his men, that's for certain," said Simon. "It could take quite some time for it to be restored."

"I agree. And for all we know, she could be dead. There might've been a power struggle, and the only reliable soul she has is Enzo to protect her."

David grunted. "If she were to die, I have no doubt those who owe her money would be rejoicing in the streets."

Jeremy shook his head. "What must it be like to be hated so much that people would prefer you dead?"

There was a knock at the front door, gentle and tentative.

Marcus smiled at the others. "Come in, Thomas." The door opened and the young man stepped inside, the farm's mastiff, Tanya, taking the opportunity to bolt. Thomas closed the door behind him to keep the warmth from the fire within the drafty walls. "How's your shoulder feeling?"

Thomas rotated the shoulder in question. "Much better, thank you. I should be good to help you tomorrow."

Jeremy smacked his hands together with a smile. "Thank God! Shoveling that shit this afternoon reminded me how much I hated it."

Thomas shifted slightly. "Um, well, about that."

13

Jeremy froze. "Please don't tell me you want to leave."

Thomas' eyes widened. "What would make you say that?"

Jeremy shook his head after a withering look from Simon. "Nothing. Never mind."

Marcus held up a hand. "You were saying?"

Thomas drew a deep breath and held it for a moment, clearly struggling with whatever message he had come to deliver. "I want to go to Paris tomorrow morning."

"What for?"

"Isabelle and I were speaking and, well, I'm sorry to say this, because, please believe me when I say, I do appreciate everything you've done for me, however the farming life is something I just can't see myself, uh, enjoying for the rest of my life. I need to use my mind, and I've never been happier than when I'm working with numbers, like I was for Mrs. Thibault."

"Despite what she does? Despite the service she provides?"

"Yes, I realize that she's not the best of people, but she isn't as horrible a soul as she appears on the surface."

Marcus smiled. "Judge not lest ye be judged."

Simon grunted. "Let he who is without sin cast the first stone."

Thomas smiled slightly. "Exactly. But Isabelle wouldn't be happy living in Paris because she'd be missing her friends and family, and she's quite accustomed to this village life."

"I am guessing from your demeanor, that fine mind

14

of yours has come up with a possible solution."

"We have, I think. We hope. What I'm proposing is that during growing season, we stay in the village and help on the farm, and during the winter months, we stay in Paris and I work for Mrs. Thibault."

Marcus' head bobbed. "It does seem like a reasonable compromise."

"You support it?"

"Absolutely. I'm not your master. You're free to do what you want, and an extra pair of hands is always welcome."

Jeremy muttered. "You're telling me."

Marcus ignored him. "Do you believe Mrs. Thibault would agree?"

Thomas sighed. "That's the question, and it's a question I need to have answered now, which is why I want to go to Paris tomorrow and find out if she would be amenable to me only working with her for perhaps five or six months of the year."

"Well, I don't see that you have any choice, young man. Take one of the horses tomorrow to Paris and get your answers, then return to us with the news."

Thomas beamed. "I'll be back the next day, I swear. Good news or bad."

Paris, Kingdom of France

Thomas Durant dismounted and handed the reins of his horse to the stable boy. The proprietor, Mr. Dezout, a man he had known all his life, smiled at him.

"Thomas! I haven't seen you in weeks." He gestured down the street toward Thomas' home. "Somebody has taken up residence in your father's house, I'm afraid. He's a beast of a man. You might have trouble getting him out."

Thomas chuckled. "That's Enzo. A friend of mine."

Dezout's eyebrows shot up. "*He's* a friend?" He frowned. "I had heard you were working for that woman, Thibault. I take it that the rumors are true then?"

Thomas nodded. "I'm afraid so."

Dezout assessed him with an extended look up and down. "You don't look very intimidating, my boy. How can you possibly collect on this woman's debts?"

"I just do the books. That's all."

Dezout frowned. "Your father might not have had a problem with what you're doing, but your mother certainly would."

"One must work."

"Aye, but surely you can do better."

"I might become a farmer."

Dezout tossed his head back, roaring with laughter. "You? A farmer?" He slapped him on the shoulder, nearly knocking him over. "You should be a jester in the King's Court with a sense of humor like that." He jerked a thumb at the horse as it was led away. "You've done well for yourself if you can afford such a fine creature."

"It's not mine. It belongs to a friend of mine. A Templar Knight."

Dezout's eyes widened. "A Templar? Huh. Well, I shall take extra care of her. But I only take payment in advance. Miss a payment, she becomes mine."

Thomas placed several coins in the man's palm. "Two nights. If I'll be longer, I'll let you know."

Dezout squeezed the coins in his hand. "Have a good evening, Thomas. My wife will be praying for you. I gave up on such nonsense too long ago to start up again now."

Thomas smiled awkwardly and hurried down the street, his heart leaping at the sight of his childhood home, warm with the glow of a fire inside, a sure sign Enzo was there.

I wonder how he'll feel about me being back early.

He was about to open the door when he stopped, instead knocking.

"Who is it?"

"It's me, Thomas. Umm, Thomas Durant."

"Thomas?" Enzo sounded genuinely excited. "Come in, boy, it's your home!"

A warmth spread through his body and he opened the door, the massive Enzo lumbering toward him, a half-eaten meal laid out on the table, the roaring fire adding its physical effects to the beast's heartfelt greetings. Thomas closed the door and extended a hand, a hand batted away, Enzo instead embracing him in both arms, lifting him from the floor and shaking him several times before putting him down.

17

"Thomas, my boy, why are you here? I thought Mrs. Thibault said to wait for word from her?"

"She did," said Thomas as he removed his traveling gear. "I come on an urgent matter, and need to ask a question of her."

Enzo frowned. "Nothing serious, I hope?"

Thomas shook his head. "Serious to me, though in a good way." His stomach rumbled at the sight of the food on the table, a large bird nearly devoured and a healthy portion of root vegetables barely touched.

"Hungry?"

"Starving."

"I wish I had more, or I'd offer you some of mine." Enzo held up a greasy finger. "But you just make yourself comfortable, and I'll be back as quick as can be."

Thomas didn't have a chance to stop him before he rushed out the door, sans coat, no doubt to fetch another meal from wherever he had sourced this one, likely meant for a family of four.

He chuckled.

He is a family of four.

He warmed his hands by the fire, allowing the heat to radiate through his chilled bones, the French winter still hanging on, then took in his home, pleased Enzo had made no noticeable changes. The door opened and Enzo lumbered back in with another bird, one leg missing.

Enzo tore a chunk of meat off the member in question, gripped in his other hand. "Sorry, hungry."

Thomas smiled as they sat around the table. "No need to apologize. There's no way I'd be able to eat all

18

of that regardless."

Enzo continued to assault the large leg. "So, what is this question you have for Mrs. Thibault?"

"I'm hoping to marry Isabelle, but she's hesitant to live in Paris, and I'm quite certain I'll make a terrible farmer. We've reached a compromise that needs Mrs. Thibault's approval."

Enzo's eyebrows rose as he wiped his mouth with the back of his hand. "Oh?"

"I need to ask if she would permit me to work for her for only half the year. Our hope is that we would live in Crécy-la-Chapelle during growing season, then we would live here during the winter. That way we both get what we want, but it can only work if Mrs. Thibault agrees."

Enzo grunted, tossing the stripped clean legbone onto the table. "When do you intend to ask her?"

"Tomorrow morning. I'll go in with you if you don't mind."

Enzo sighed, staring at him. "There's something you should know."

Thomas tensed, Enzo's tone heavy. "What?"

"Things have changed since you left."

"How?"

"Something is wrong. I don't know what, but it's something."

Thomas regarded Enzo. "I'm going to need more than that, my friend."

Enzo grunted, then tore off a wing. "Some of our debtors have stopped making their payments. Things were chaotic for a few weeks after that business we were mixed up in, but it calmed down fairly quickly.

Mrs. Thibault and a few of the others came to an agreement to carve up Pequin's territory, and things were pretty peaceful after that." He bit off a chunk and chewed, his mouth open as he continued. "At first, we thought somebody was trying to steal our business, you know, not sticking to the agreement, but usually that involves paying off someone's debt, and then the payments go to them. But it's nothing like that, you see? They didn't pay off their debts with money borrowed from another, they just stopped paying. And when I go around and visit them, they swear they don't have any money, that they'll make the payments, but they don't. Even when I threaten them, they don't, but I know they've got money."

"How?"

"Because they're always drunk, or at least look like they were the night before."

Thomas frowned. "That seems odd. Are they problems?"

Enzo shook his head. "No, these are the good ones."

"How many?"

"Not a lot. Half a dozen, but it keeps growing, a new one each week. Mrs. Thibault is getting concerned. Wants me to figure it out." Enzo shrugged. "You know me, Thomas, I'm not very smart." His face brightened. "Maybe you could figure it out! If you did, I bet you she'd agree to your plan!"

Thomas chewed his cheek, unable to think of any way out of Enzo's idea. If Thibault were in a foul mood, there would be no point in asking her his question. And Enzo was right. If he could figure out the problem, it could put her in a better mood, and him in her good graces.

Unless the answer proved worse than the mystery.

Thibault Residence
Paris, Kingdom of France

"Enzo, you're a little late today."

Simone Thibault's enforcer didn't appear contrite, instead the smile on his twisted face suggested his mood was a happy one. "I'm sorry, ma'am, but I had a visitor show up last night."

Her eyebrows rose in surprise. "Visitor? I wasn't aware you had any friends."

"Just the one, ma'am."

She eyed him skeptically. "And just who is this friend?"

Enzo stepped his massive frame aside, revealing the impossibly slight Thomas standing behind him.

"Thomas!" She was surprised at how genuinely happy she was to see the young man. Her husband had died before they had children, and over the past few months, she had come to think of Thomas as her own son. "Come in, Thomas, come in!" She pointed to a chair and he sat. "Weren't you supposed to wait for my message before you returned?"

Thomas' head dropped to his chest. There was no hiding contrition with him. "Yes, ma'am, however no message came, and I had a pressing matter I needed to discuss with you."

"Things were quite on edge here for some weeks, however those of us in the business, shall we say, came to an agreement and carved up Pequin's territory. Things have been stable since then, however we've run into another issue."

"The matter of your debtors not paying?"

She eyed her enforcer. "I see Enzo has told you."

"He told me a little of what's been going on."

Enzo stared at his shoes. "I'm sorry, ma'am, if you didn't want me to, but I felt that if anyone could be trusted, it would be Thomas."

She smiled at him. "Not to worry. I trust Thomas implicitly, and in fact, I could use his help."

Thomas' eyes widened. "I'm not sure how I can help in these matters. You know me, I just do the numbers. I rarely go out."

"This is true. However, you and Enzo are the only ones I trust in my life, and I can't exactly send Enzo out discreetly."

"What is it that you want me to do?"

"I want you to find out why men who always paid on time, are no longer paying, yet appear to still be earning the money they used to. I want you to find out where that money is going."

"But I'm supposed to return to Crécy-la-Chapelle today."

"Why would you come here for only one day? Oh, that's right. You had a pressing matter to discuss with me. What is it?"

"Well, I'm hoping to marry Isabelle Leblanc."

Her chest tightened with the word she was about to lose her protege. "I see. Has a date been set?"

"Oh no, no. We're not even engaged yet. We're merely discussing the future, and I've come to feel that I can't be happy as a farmer, and she believes she'd be equally unhappy living in Paris."

She felt a strange satisfaction with that. "Then I can't see how it could possibly work."

"Well, we figured out a way we believe we can both be happy."

Her eyebrows shot up. "Oh?"

"Yes. Umm, what we are proposing is that during the growing season, we stay in the village, and I will help with the farm, and then in the offseason, we stay in Paris and I work for you."

She leaned back, folding her arms. "An interesting idea that. You both get what you want for half the year, and the other half each is miserable."

Thomas frowned. "I hadn't thought of it that way."

"Perhaps you should."

He stared at his hands for a moment then shook his head. "No, I don't believe so. We love each other. We'll both be able to tolerate the halves of the year that aren't the most desirable. Knowing that there is an end coming up so soon should tide us over."

"And I suppose you're here to ask me if I would be agreeable to this situation."

"Yes, ma'am."

She stared at him, striving to give him the impression that she was struggling with the decision, though she had already made it. If she said no, she could lose him forever, and things had run so much more smoothly since he'd been here. He was the first person she had encountered to have an aptitude with numbers better than her own. She had always managed the business side of things. Her business had grown from beyond anything her husband had accomplished when he was in charge, and it simply wasn't manageable anymore with just her and Enzo along with a few hired

24

mounds of muscle when it was needed. Thomas had been a godsend. Having him only five or six months of the year was better than none, and replacing him would be next to impossible in these slums. She sighed. "I suppose. It's a tremendous inconvenience, however I'm willing to make the sacrifice. But you'll have to work doubly hard when you are here."

Thomas beamed. "Of course! Absolutely!"

"Good, but I have one condition."

The boy appeared to tense. "What?"

"Before you return to Crécy-la-Chapelle, you must discover the truth about what is happening with my debtors."

Outside Chapon Family Bakery
Paris, Kingdom of France

Thomas had left Thibault's office not an hour after arriving, and had confirmed that one of her debtors who had missed his last two payments, Jacques Chapon, had been in his bakery all day. Thomas was convinced that whatever the man was spending his money on was nothing that occurred during the day, otherwise the man's business would have collapsed by now.

Though not everything was running smoothly.

He had heard grumblings from some of the customers coming out of the bakery indicating the full selection normally available wasn't, and that those that had come first thing in the morning had been forced to return because he hadn't been open.

This lent credence to his theory that whatever was happening was happening at night, causing Chapon to be late in prepping the ovens. Bakers were up long before the crack of dawn baking their wares for those who *did* wake up at the crack of dawn in search of them. Something was going on here, and it was going on at night, though if he truly trusted his assumption, he would be warm right now, in front of a fire at his family home. But he couldn't risk being wrong, and the sooner he discovered the truth, the sooner he could return to Crécy-la-Chapelle and Isabelle.

Oh Lord, how he loved her. He had never felt this way about anyone, had never known love like this before, had never known it was possible. The only love he had been exposed to was that of his parents. He had vague recollections of the love his mother and father had shared, though they had hidden it so well, he couldn't believe it was possibly as strong as what he had with Isabelle. Yet he was certain the love his parents had was true, his father's devastation over her death still unforgettable, as if it had happened just yesterday.

And now he was certain he would freeze for at least an hour if not more. Chapon was sure to be cleaning up things from a busy day, then sitting for his evening meal with his family. He debated returning to the house, warming up, getting something to eat, then coming back in an hour. He was quite sure nothing would happen between now and then. The man couldn't exactly spend his money within his own four walls. Whatever he was spending it on, had to be happening somewhere else. Thibault had thought the man drunk, or at least hungover, and that suggested that after a day's work, the man was indulging a little too much.

But he had met Mrs. Chapon, and she was a pious woman who would never permit excessive drinking under her roof, which raised the question, would she tolerate him returning home drunk at night? The woman was well aware of the loan Chapon had with Thibault, because according to Enzo, they had both come into the office, hat in hand, after an accident left their ovens damaged, and they had to be rebuilt to save the business. They had been desperate, with no choice but to go to a woman like Thibault, and they had diligently made their payments since, slowly working down their debt for over a year. Yet something had changed, and he had a feeling it was a change of which Mrs. Chapon wasn't aware. Her husband was up to something that could cost them their business, as it was the collateral for the loan.

He stamped his feet in an attempt to stimulate a little bit of warmth. He thanked the Good Lord that spring would arrive eventually, but if he had to stand out here too long, he'd freeze to death. He paced back and forth in the alley, boosting his circulation, then leaned against the wall opposite the one he had been holding vigil next to, no longer as concerned with being spotted in the dark.

And he smiled.

There was a fire on the opposite side of the stone against which he now leaned. Heat radiated through the rock, then his jacket, and finally his skin. Within minutes, he felt rejuvenated. With the torture of the cold gone and the prospects for the evening looking up, it unfortunately allowed him to focus on the hunger in his belly. If he was to be here for the rest of the night, he must eat something. He knew the neighborhood well, and there was a place he could get food a hundred paces from here. He debated what to do, but one final angry growl from his stomach had his mind made up.

He rushed toward the tavern and went inside. He ate his hearty meal as quickly as he could, shoveling the thick stew and a crusty bread into his mouth while washing it down with a cup of wine. He thanked the proprietor, who he also had known for years, and returned to his post, praying that the precious quarter-hour he had been gone hadn't been enough for the man to leave.

He leaned against the warm stone, and from his vantage point, stared at the bakery, all evidence of life gone dark. He settled in for the long haul, and his thoughts soon drifted to Isabelle and the farm. He should be there by now, and he had no doubt they were worried about him. Tomorrow, he'd send a message via the Templar network to put their mind at ease if he weren't already on his way there. Hopefully, whatever Chapon was up to would be determined tonight, and his business for Thibault would be concluded, making the message unnecessary.

After what felt like hours, he stood straight, his heart pounding at the sight of the front door opening, Chapon stepping outside. The man looked both ways, as if to make certain he wasn't being watched, then hurried down the street. Thomas kept as close as he dared, not wanting to risk being spotted, for though he wasn't as visible as the massive Enzo might be, Chapon was a man he had known for years, and was a man who knew he had recently begun working for Thibault. There'd be no doubt why he was here at this time of night should he be spotted.

He kept to the opposite side of the street, ducking in alleyways and doorways as much as he could, avoiding any torchlight if possible. He followed the man for about ten minutes then stopped when Chapon darted into an alley. Thomas sprinted across the road and peered around the corner to find Chapon rapping on a door in, if he wasn't mistaken, a coded fashion.

Three raps, then one, then two.

A Judas hole opened, a dull glow shining through for a moment before it slid shut, then the door opened. Chapon disappeared inside. Thomas examined his surroundings, this part of the neighborhood at the outer range of where he usually roamed. The front of the building suggested it was a clothing shop, something rather unusual for this area, most unable to afford such things—most clothes were handmade, and passed down until they could no longer be worn, the scraps used to repair those still deemed wearable.

He stared in the darkness at the building, wondering why there was no indication of life. He struggled to focus his eyes, searching for any light, anything that might indicate something going on inside, yet could see nothing. Then his eyes widened. There *was* light.

A dull glow from underneath.

They're in the basement!

A foot scraped behind him and he spun, his heart racing.

"Now, what do you think you're doing?"

His eyes bulged at the sight of a burly man, a club in his hand. "N-nothing. I'm just heading home."

"Are you now." The man raised the club high above his head.

De Rancourt Family Farm
Crécy-la-Chapelle, Kingdom of France

"I'm concerned."

Sir Marcus regarded Isabelle as Lady Joanne wrapped an arm over the young girl's shoulders. "As am I," she said.

Isabelle stared at him. "Do you think something has happened to him, or do you think he's decided to stay in Paris and forget me?"

Joanne squeezed her tight. "Oh, you poor dear. I'm sure it's nothing of the sort. He was probably just delayed leaving, and decided it was best not to risk traveling in the dark. He'll be here tomorrow."

Marcus smiled reassuringly. "I agree with Lady Joanne. It's too early to fear the worst, though it is unlike him to be late, and definitely not like him to not send word."

"But how would he get word to us?" asked Isabelle.

"He could use the Templar messenger network. All he would have to do is go to the Fortress and leave a message for me, and they would have brought it here."

"Would he think to do that?"

Simon grunted. "He would think to do it, though I don't know if he would have the courage."

She shot daggers at him then returned her attention to Marcus. "If he's not here in the morning, then I want to go to Paris and search for him. If he's decided to stay, then I need to hear it from his own lips."

Marcus frowned. "If he's not here tonight, then he

31

won't be here in the morning. He wouldn't be foolish enough to travel in the dark."

She rose. "Then we should leave now."

"He isn't foolish enough to travel at this hour, nor are we. If you wish, we will take you to Paris tomorrow. If we're lucky, we'll encounter him on our way there."

"Thank you."

Marcus left the house and walked up to the barracks with Simon, Tanya dutifully at his side.

"What do you think is going on?"

He glanced at Simon. "My gut tells me the boy has cold feet and has taken the easy way out of ending the relationship with young Isabelle."

Simon growled. "If that's the case, then he better pray I don't find him. I'll tear his balls off for hurting that young girl."

Marcus chuckled. "I think you'll have to get in line."

"One nut each it is."

They entered the barracks and his squires rose as Tanya curled up by the fire.

"Any word on Thomas?" asked Jeremy.

Marcus shook his head. "No. We'll be heading to Paris in the morning with Isabelle to find him."

David's eyes widened. "With Isabelle? Is that wise?"

"She's convinced he's decided to end the relationship. If so, she wants to hear it from his own lips."

Jeremy clenched his fists. "Well, if that little shit is taking the cowardly way out of ending a relationship with that lovely young woman, I'll cut his balls off."

Simon glanced at Marcus. "There appears to be a lot of demand for the boy's balls."

Unknown Location

Thomas woke, his head pounding. He reached up to grab the pain, but found his hands were bound behind him. He opened his eyes and peered into the haze in front of him, blinking several times as he struggled to bring his surroundings into focus. It took several moments for him to realize it had nothing to do with his vision, and everything to do with a thick smoky haze surrounding him, accompanied by an odd odor he had never before smelled.

"He's awake."

Thomas flinched then turned toward the voice, a mere form in the shadows behind him.

"What's your name, boy?" asked another voice.

He wasn't sure if he should answer. In fact, he was certain he shouldn't answer, at least not with the truth. "Umm, Gilles?"

"You don't sound too certain about that."

"His name is Thomas Durant."

Thomas gulped at the truth revealed by another voice, but not just any voice. It was a voice he recognized as that of Chapon.

"So, why are you following this man?"

"I-I wasn't."

"You were standing outside his bakery all day, and then the moment he left, you followed. You expect me to believe that was just a coincidence?"

Thomas wasn't certain what to say, though once the words that came from his mouth were finished, he was quite certain it wasn't that. "Umm, I enjoy the smell of freshly baked goods?"

Everyone in the room laughed, including several he couldn't see, the only light from a fire behind him and several candles, all placed in close proximity to him.

"Your sense of humor could get you killed, boy."

His heart raced. "Why? Why would you kill me? I've done nothing wrong!"

"Oh, you've done something wrong."

"What?"

"Boy, you stuck your nose into business that wasn't yours."

"But I don't even know what business that is! I don't know what you're talking about!"

"I think you do. Why else would you have been following Mr. Chapon?"

He had to tell the truth. At least some of it. His life was at stake here, and besides, he was quite certain Enzo could protect Thibault. Right now, he had to survive not only for his own sake, but for Isabelle's. He sighed. "I was told to."

"Who told you to?"

A thought occurred to him and he jerked his chin toward Chapon, hoping to deflect some of the anger in the room toward someone else. "Ask him. He knows."

"I don't know what he's talking about!" protested Chapon.

"Yes, you do! Why don't you tell them the truth, or are you afraid that it might get you in trouble? I was only doing my job, but you, you weren't."

"I swear, I don't know what he's talking about!"

The man who appeared in charge emerged from the

shadows and approached Chapon. Thomas still couldn't see the man's face, and had no idea who he could possibly be. "I think you know exactly what he's talking about."

"I swear! I swear, I don't know!"

Thomas suppressed a smile at the terror in Chapon's voice. The attention had been taken away from him, and was now solely focused where it should be. Though after mere moments of relief, guilt swept through him. Chapon was a good man, but whatever he was mixed up in was evidently something nefarious.

Perhaps he's not as good a man as everyone thinks.

"Tell us now, or I'll cut your tongue out so that whatever it is that's brought attention to this place can never be spoken of again."

Thomas heard Chapon sigh. "Very well. He works for Mrs. Thibault."

"Who's that?"

"A money lender."

"So, you owe her money then?"

"Yes."

"And let me guess. You haven't been making your payments."

"No."

"How many have you missed?"

"Two so far."

"Yet you come here almost every night."

"I-I can't help myself. I try to resist, but by the time my wife falls asleep, I'm shaking, and I can't stop the shaking until I come here."

"I warned you of this. I said to come no more than once a week." The man sighed. "I blame myself. I'm

35

too trusting a person. I believe in the goodness, the basic goodness of all men. I believe it when they tell me that they can keep things under control, that they can handle themselves. But with you, clearly I was wrong. I'm too trusting a soul."

"You're a good man, sir, and I'm sorry for disappointing you."

"Oh, you've done more than disappoint me. You've endangered my business. You've brought the attention of this Mrs. Thibault to these premises."

"I swear I'll pay back what I owe her, and then she'll have no more interest in me, therefore no more interest in your affairs."

"But how can you possibly pay her back, especially if your business is suffering? My people tell me that your bakery opened late today, and it wasn't the first time this week that it did. You're neglecting your duties, you're neglecting your business, which means your income will suffer."

"I-I might be able to borrow money from someone else."

"Oh, yes, the ever-wise plan to pay off one debt by taking on another. Only fools borrow money they can't afford to make the payments on."

"But I always made the payments! I was always on time. Just ask Thomas. He'll tell you."

Thomas felt compelled to defend the man. "It's true, sir. He was always on time. Never a day late, never a *denier* short. He only missed the last two payments."

"And how long have you been coming here?"

"I'm not sure," replied Chapon. "A month, perhaps."

"Yes, and already you're two weeks behind. I think

36

it's clear you cannot handle what we offer here. I think our relationship is over."

This declaration sent Chapon into a panic. "No, please! I need it! I can't live without it! Please, give me a second chance! I'll cut back, I swear. Just twice a week. Three times a week."

"I don't believe you are capable."

"No, I swear I can do it. I can handle it."

The boss sighed. "Again, perhaps I'm too trusting a soul, but I'm willing to help you. From now on, you can only stay for an hour each night. That should help keep things under control, but you must bring your account up to date with Mrs. Thibault."

"I will! I swear, I will!"

"You better, however you are no longer the problem, merely the cause of it, and anything I do to you won't solve it." He turned toward Thomas. "You, my boy, are the problem that Mr. Chapon created."

Thomas gulped. "I-I'm not a problem. I swear I won't tell anybody anything. I don't even know what I would tell them. I haven't seen anything. I don't know who you are. I haven't seen your face. I'm not even sure where I am."

"Don't play stupid with me, boy. You know exactly where you are, and even if you didn't, you know where this fool went. Him, I trust not to tell anyone anything because he's too scared of what could happen to him, and besides, he already knows where we are. You, on the other hand, will run back to Mrs. Thibault and tell her exactly what you saw here tonight, and even if you didn't, she'll demand to know what happened." He paced in front of him, each heel-turn excruciating to Thomas' ears. "No, we can't have you running about telling everyone what you saw."

Thomas was desperate now. "I'm leaving Paris tomorrow. Just let me go. I swear I won't tell anybody anything, and I'll never come back."

"I'm afraid that's not good enough." The man sighed. "I'm afraid we have no choice but to kill you."

"I wouldn't do that," said Chapon. "He has friends. Templars."

The man paused. "Templars?"

"Yes. Someone named Sir Marcus. I don't remember the last name."

The man turned toward Thomas. "What is this knight's name?"

Revealing the truth might be the only thing that could save his life. "His name is Sir Marcus de Rancourt."

"And he's a friend?"

"A good friend. He's invited me to live on his farm."

"A Templar who lives on a farm?"

"It's a long story. He has special dispensation due to a family situation."

The man sighed. "This could be a problem." He snapped his fingers. "Give it to him."

Thomas heard footfalls behind him then something was shoved in his mouth. A hand clamped over his jaw and his nose was pinched. He held his breath but was finally forced to inhale.

And he discovered the source of the odd odor.

Durant Residence
Paris, Kingdom of France

Enzo wasn't sure if he should be concerned. Thomas hadn't returned yet. He was watching Chapon, and if whatever the baker was spending his money on took place after dark, then Thomas wouldn't be expected to have yet returned. However, it was very late. The sun would be rising in a couple of hours, and he hadn't slept a wink. Instead, he sat tending the fire, listening for any telltale signs of the young man's return.

He couldn't remember when he had started thinking of Thomas as a friend, but he now did. Perhaps it was because the boy didn't treat him like a freak. Everyone he encountered was scared of him, even when he was pleasant with them. His size and twisted face had him lonely most of his days. He had no family to speak of, having been abandoned by his parents long before his earliest memories, likely because of his freakish nature and the embarrassment it brought them. He had survived, his brawn of use to the worst of those who made the slums of Paris their home.

He didn't enjoy what he did, especially when he was forced to hurt people, though that wasn't entirely true. He did enjoy hurting bad people. That always brought a smile to his face, but hurting people like Chapon simply because they had failed to make a payment, was never a source of pleasure for him. With no family and no friends, Thibault was all he had, and she did treat him well enough, better than any employer before.

And then Thomas entered his life.

39

He was the complete opposite of him—all brains and no brawn. If there were a muscle on the boy's body, it was in the hand that held his pen. It meant he needn't worry about him at all. The boy could never hurt him physically, and after a few weeks of working for Thibault, the boy no longer seemed intimidated by the size or appearance of her enforcer. In fact, they had partaken in many pleasant discussions, though he found he was quite often just listening, as Thomas was far more intelligent than he could ever dream of being. And because Thomas treated him with respect, there was only one way he could repay him, and it was through protecting the boy.

And yet, sitting here, he felt helpless. There was nothing he could do. Thibault's orders had been clear. He wasn't to go near the baker. It had to be Thomas, otherwise Chapon might become suspicious, and this problem was greater than one late debtor.

He stared into the fire, his eyes growing heavy, and did something he rarely did.

Prayed.

40

Thibault Residence
Paris, Kingdom of France

"What do you mean he never came home?"

"Just that, ma'am. I waited up all night and he never came."

Thibault frowned. "So, you never saw him after he left here?"

Enzo shook his head. "No."

"That's not like him."

"I'm worried, ma'am. I think something may have happened to him. Perhaps Mr. Chapon caught him."

"Chapon is a coward. He would never dare touch Thomas. He knows he works for me."

"We have to do something, ma'am. He's my friend."

She regarded him for a moment. He was right. Thomas not coming home meant something had gone wrong. Though perhaps not. Perhaps whatever he had discovered was still ongoing. After all, she had heard reports that the bakery had opened late at least twice this week, and that likely meant whatever Chapon was up to was occurring late at night. She smiled slightly. "Perhaps we're being a little hasty. Go to the bakery and see if Mr. Chapon is there."

"Do you want me to bring him back?"

"No, just find out if he's there. If he is, then we know Thomas is missing. If he isn't, then he might simply still be following Mr. Chapon."

"Yes, ma'am. I'll check back at the house as well."

"Do that."

41

He hurried down the stairs as fast as she had ever heard him, the poor man clearly distraught. It was an interesting thing to see him expressing emotions other than anger. It was the first time she had ever had a sense he could genuinely care for something or someone. She trusted the man with her life. She even liked him despite his grotesque appearance, though she didn't really consider him a friend. He wasn't someone she could have a conversation with that didn't involve business and giving him orders, though the pit in her stomach at his despair, at his concern, had her thinking perhaps she did indeed care about this beast of a man that protected her life day in and day out. Though if her feelings for Enzo weren't clear, they were for Thomas, and she genuinely feared for his safety, for if anything had happened to him, it would be her fault, as she had sent him on what might have been his final task for her.

A task that might have cost the poor boy his life.

Leblanc Residence
Crécy-la-Chapelle, Kingdom of France

Isabelle finished packing her small bag with the essentials she would need for one day in Paris, then joined her parents at the kitchen table, her mother putting her breakfast in front of her before sitting back down, a frown deeply creasing her face.

"I really think this is a foolish thing you're up to."

Isabelle swallowed a forkful of egg. "I have to know, Mother. I have to know why he didn't come back."

"You may not like the answer."

Isabelle put her fork down. "If I don't go now, I'll spend the rest of my life wondering why. And you're assuming the worst. You're assuming that he's actually not coming back by choice, that he's decided he doesn't want to be with me. Maybe something happened to him."

Her father gave her a look. "You have the mind of a child."

She bristled. "What do you mean by that?"

"You would rather something to have happened to him, than to have had him simply decide he didn't want to pursue this relationship you two have. You need to get your priorities straight, girl. If he's decided he doesn't want to be with you, then let it be. Don't beg him to be in a relationship he doesn't want to be in."

"But father, I love him!"

"Yes, and I have no doubt that he loves you, but I've seen the boy working the farm. He is no farmer, and never will be."

"But we figured out a compromise!"

"Yes, and surprisingly, I believe it's a good compromise, though I'd hate to see you living in that hellhole of a city for half the year, especially during the winter."

"But he has a home there. A fine home."

He gave her a look. "A fine home?"

She frowned. "Well, it's a home. It's a roof. It's walls. It's warmth. It's shelter in a neighborhood where we could feed ourselves with the money he earns."

"And what if something goes wrong?" asked her mother. "Sir Marcus won't be there to protect you."

"No, but Enzo will be, and then there are always the Templars."

Her father grunted. "If Enzo is who I think he is, he's a criminal, just like that woman your future husband works for."

Her mother sighed heavily, shaking her head. "I can't believe you're going to marry a criminal."

"Thomas is not a criminal!" she screamed, jumping from her seat.

"He is if he works for her," said her father.

"You two just don't understand! I'm going to Paris! I'm going to find Thomas and I'm going to marry Thomas and then I'm moving out of here, and you better be careful what you say about him, or it won't be just six months of the year you won't be seeing me, it'll be all twelve!"

THE BLACK SCOURGE

Outside Chapon Family Bakery
Paris, Kingdom of France

Enzo stood across the street from the bakery, his heart hammering as a combination of rage and fear for his friend consumed him. He clenched his fists as he heard Chapon, his voice cheerily calling out to his customers as they entered his shop. He had already inquired in a shop adjacent to the bakery and confirmed that it had indeed opened on time with a full selection of its regular offerings. Whatever had happened last night with Chapon hadn't prevented him from returning home. Yet Thomas was nowhere to be seen. He had already searched the alleyways or any other place he could think of that Thomas might be watching from, but had come up empty. It was everything he could do not to cross the street and beat the truth out of the baker, but he had his orders.

He headed back to Thomas' home and found it as empty as he had left it this morning. He cursed, slamming a fist down on the table, the solid top snapping off the legs.

There was no doubt now. Something had definitely happened to Thomas.

De Rancourt Family Farm
Crécy-la-Chapelle, Kingdom of France

Marcus headed up the hill toward the barracks, having just finished breakfast with the family and saying his goodbyes to his niece and nephew and their ward Pierre. The doors of the barn were open, and he could see David and Jeremy preparing three horses for their journey. "Everything ready?"

David nodded. "Yes, sir. We've provisioned you for two days, just in case. You can reequip at the Fortress if necessary."

"Excellent. I'm not sure how long we'll be. If Thomas is simply cowering in his home, then we could be back tomorrow."

"With his balls," said Simon as he stepped from the barracks in full Templar regalia.

Jeremy looked at him. "Huh?"

Marcus chuckled. "Never mind. If this is simply a misunderstanding, we might be back tomorrow, but if something has indeed happened to him, I'm not sure how long we'll be. I'm sure young Isabelle won't let us rest until we either find him or what became of him. If it looks like we'll be there more than three days, I'll send word."

"Do you want us to join you?" asked David, the hope in his voice clearly indicating his preference to staying on the farm.

"No. Stay here unless you hear differently from me. If you don't hear from me in five days, then send word to the Fortress and let them know what has happened so they can begin a search."

David frowned. "Do you expect trouble?"

"No. At the moment, I expect to find a young man who has taken the easy way out by abandoning the woman he loves out of fear of a future he'll hate."

Thibault Residence
Paris, Kingdom of France

Enzo hauled Chapon up the stairs and shoved him through the door to Thibault's office. After reporting the man was at the bakery, she had ordered him to collect the man for questioning.

"Be gentle about it," she had said. "We don't need any untoward attention being drawn to us."

He had been disappointed at the guidance given, though he had to obey her orders, politely requesting the man accompany him. Mrs. Chapon hadn't been pleased, but was fully aware of who he was and who he represented. She had wisely held her tongue.

"Mr. Chapon, have a seat, please."

This was something not generally offered to the man, and his trembling increased as he sat with his hands clasped in his lap, his entire body shaking with what appeared to be more than just fear.

"I have a question for you."

"Yes, ma'am, anything. I'm happy to help." Chapon was a bundle of nerves, his voice aquiver.

"You know the young man that works for me, Thomas Durant?"

Enzo noticed the man's face go pale.

He knows something.

"Yes, ma'am, I know Thomas. He grew up in our neighborhood."

"Then he's a neighbor of yours. A good neighbor."

"Yes, ma'am."

"And did you know his parents?"

"Yes, ma'am. They were good people."

"So, you wouldn't want anything untoward to happen to him, would you?"

"Of-of course not, ma'am."

She smiled slightly. "Of course, not. You're a good man."

"Thank you, ma'am."

"So, as a good man, I want you to answer me one question."

"Anything, ma'am."

She leaned forward, staring directly into his eyes. "What have you done with Thomas?"

His eyes bulged. "Ma'am?"

"It's a simple question. What have you done with Thomas?"

"N-nothing! I swear!"

She sat back in her chair and folded her arms. "If you haven't done something to him, then you know who did. I want you to tell me what happened to Thomas, or I'm going to leave you alone in this room with Enzo."

Enzo inhaled deeply, expanding his already impressive chest, and added a low rumbling growl.

Chapon cringed, the desired effect achieved. "Please, ma'am! I swear I didn't do anything to him!"

"I believe you. I don't believe it's in your nature to hurt somebody, which means somebody else did. Perhaps whoever you've been giving my money to."

If Chapon's face could become paler, it did in that moment. "I swear I didn't do anything to him!"

Thibault stared at the man. "Interesting. I believe

49

you're more scared of them than you are Enzo, and that's saying something." Chapon's hands trembled uncontrollably, yet he remained silent. "I'll make you an offer. You tell me where Thomas is, and I'll forgive your late payments."

His eyes shot wide and he gripped the arms of his chair. "I-I…" His shoulders slumped and he fell silent.

Thibault stared at him, surprised. "You're refusing my offer?"

He shook his head vigorously. "No, ma'am, I'm not." He sighed. "You don't know what you're asking me to do."

"I'm asking you to help save a young man's life. A young man that grew up in your neighborhood, a young man whose parents you knew, a young man who's done nothing wrong."

He stared at the floor. "But, ma'am, if I tell you, it will mean certain death for me and my family."

"Why? Who is it that has you so terrified you would risk being left alone with Enzo?"

Tears rolled down the man's cheeks and the distinct odor of urine filled the room, yet he remained silent.

Thibault beckoned Enzo with a single finger. "Enzo, persuade our friend to speak."

Chapon leaped from his chair, waving his hands in front of him as he retreated into the far corner. "No, please!"

"Then tell me what I want to know. Who is it that you're so afraid of?"

Chapon stared at her. "If I tell you, you can't tell anyone that you found out from me."

"Of course."

He stared at the floor, but still said nothing.

"Tell me now, or Enzo tears your arm off. I'll let you choose which one."

More urine ran down the man's leg, draining him of any remaining resistance. "Fine." He lifted his head and met her stare. "It's the Templars."

Outside Thibault Residence
Paris, Kingdom of France

Chapon hurried from Thibault's office, his heart palpitating over the fact he had just revealed the terrible truth to the very people to whom he had been told not to say anything. The moment he had revealed it was Templars, she had been scared and ended the meeting. He dared not bring up her offer, though he prayed that if his life were now at risk, she would honor her promise of forgiveness over the missed payments. It would make a huge difference to their lives, though only should they have them to enjoy if this untenable situation passed.

The worst thing about this was that it was all his fault. He had let things get out of control. Life in Paris was misery, at least in the slums, and he had it better off than most. His bakery was as successful as one could expect in a neighborhood where people could barely afford his wares on a good day. Many people's livelihoods took a hit during the winter months, so he quite often was paid not in coin, but in bartered goods. He didn't mind it. It was just the way things were. It had always been this way, and always would be. Sometimes those paid in coin like him, would pay him in the same, and those who weren't, sometimes paid with eggs or whatever it was they had to barter. And his family needed eggs. It was a system that worked, and it kept his family clothed and fed, with a roof over their heads. He loved his wife, he loved his children, and he hated himself for having put it all at risk.

I'm never going back there.

Yet he had said that countless times before, though never from a position such as he now found himself. He was in trouble. He was in danger. He had to figure a way out of this, yet what could he do against the Templar Order? They were powerful. They were rich.

And they were ruthless.

He found it ironic that Thomas Durant, who apparently had Templar friends and was the only person who might put in a good word for him, was now a prisoner.

Thanks to him.

He headed down the alleyway and through the rear entrance of his residence rather than walk through the business with his urine-stained pants. He quickly stripped them off, washed as best he could with the water from the now cold basin, then put on a fresh pair, wondering how he would explain to his wife what had happened without revealing the truth. But he wasn't certain how he could avoid it. She knew Enzo had come to the shop that morning. She knew where he had gone. She would be asking questions as it was her right to do.

Perhaps he could tell her a partial truth that fit with the facts. He could tell her he had been threatened over being late on his payments, and Enzo had scared the piss out of him.

Literally.

He cursed as he remembered she didn't know they were two weeks behind on their payments. He sighed. This entire situation was ridiculous. He had to tell her, as he would need her help. It was already difficult after just half a day of not indulging. If he were to go a lifetime, he wasn't sure how he could survive.

He eyed their bed and its four posts, a prized possession for any home.

Perhaps she could tie me to the bed until it passed.

He assumed it was like any other indulgence. Take it away, and it was painful, though in time, it would pass.

"Jacques, is that you? Are you home?"

He flinched at his wife calling his name through the door that separated the business from the residence. "Yes, I'll be there in a moment."

"Well, hurry up. We've got a line."

"Give me a moment!" he snapped, immediately regretting his tone.

Tonight, you tell her everything.

En route to Paris, Kingdom of France

"I think I could make quite a lovely go of it. I've always grown up thinking of Paris as a vile place filled with nothing but criminals and people who would as soon cut your throat as they would say good day, but that can't be true, can it? How could an entire city possibly be filled with the vilest of humanity?"

Simon grunted. "You've obviously never been to Acre."

Isabelle glanced at him. "Where?"

Marcus gave his sergeant a look. "Ignore him. He's just being difficult. You are correct, however. I've found most people in Paris to be quite pleasant. Remember, Thomas is from Paris, and if he is an example of the average person there, then I think you'll find yourself in good company. You simply have to be more careful. In any city, there are many desperate people, and desperate people can do unexpected things they would never dream of doing if they or their children weren't starving. And because Thomas is now much better off than most of his neighbors, you'll find that jealousy is a factor while you're there. Be careful. Don't go out after dark, and never flaunt what you have and others don't."

"Wise advice at the best of times, I'm sure, but you've seen Thomas' house. Is it a fine house?"

Marcus chose his words carefully. "It's a respectable home. A different style than what you're used to on the farm, however I think you'll find it quite adequate."

"Oh, I think we will be blissfully happy there."

"I think you can be if you learn to adjust."

They rode in silence for several moments when she turned in her saddle. "I think I need to learn to defend myself." She gestured at his sword. "Can you teach me how to use that?"

His eyes shot wide as did Simon's. "Excuse me?"

"Can you teach me how to use your sword?"

"I'm not sure you'd be able to even pick it up."

"I'm strong."

"I have no doubt, but many men would struggle."

"Let's settle this." She brought her horse to a stop and dismounted. Marcus shrugged at Simon and they both came to a halt and dismounted. Marcus drew his sword, handing it to her. She gripped it with both hands.

"Do you have it?" he asked.

"Of course I have it."

He let go and the tip of the blade immediately dropped to the ground, embedding in the frozen mud. Simon chuckled and she glared, silencing him.

She groaned, struggling against the weight, and the sword slowly lifted, her face beet red, her arms trembling. She raised it, pointing it directly at his chest.

Marcus was impressed. "I didn't think you had it in you."

"Take it before you prove your words false!" she muttered.

He laughed and took the sword from her, returning it to its sheath. He drew his dagger, flipping it in the air and catching it by the flat of the blade. He held it out to her. "Perhaps I could show you how to use this instead."

Her eyes bulged. "You didn't tell me you had one of those!"

Simon roared with laughter. "You better not teach her how to use that. You're liable to be her first victim."

She took the blade. "Will you teach me how to use it?"

"If you wish, though I'm not certain how your father would feel about that."

She growled. "I don't care what he thinks. He thinks Thomas is a criminal."

Marcus held his tongue for a moment. "I suppose it would depend on how you defined criminal."

She gasped. "You believe he is?"

"No, not in how I define criminal. He doesn't hurt people. He doesn't steal from people, though he does work for a woman who, through her actions, does."

She held up the knife. "If you kill someone with this knife, is the knife to blame, or the person who wielded it?"

He smiled. "You're a wise woman, Miss Isabelle. Yes, perhaps Thomas is merely a tool used by Mrs. Thibault." He nodded at the dagger. "I will teach you how to use this weapon, but you must promise me that you'll never use your knowledge in anger. Like I said, jealousy and desperation make people do strange things, including saying hurtful things. People know what Thomas does and who he works for, and they'll resent it. They may take out their frustrations on you, likely saying horrible things to provoke a reaction from you. If you carry a knife, you must control your anger, otherwise you might lash out and hurt someone or worse, kill a truly innocent person merely for what they say about your future husband's questionable choice of profession."

"I promise."

"Very well, then this is as good a time as any to rest the horses and give you your first lesson."

She smiled. "I agree. What's my first lesson?"

"How to hold a knife."

She looked down at the blade in her hand. "There's more than one way?"

Simon grunted. "Yes, there are two ways. The right way, and the wrong way. Guess which way you're holding it."

Thibault Residence
Paris, Kingdom of France

Thibault sat at her desk, saying nothing. Enzo stood in the corner as he usually did, giving him a clear view of the stairway leading to her office, the only way in besides the window immediately to his left. The very notion it was Templars than Chapon was so terrified of, had her scared as well. She didn't trust the Templars. Any organization that had so much money and wealth, yet claimed to be poor soldiers of Christ, were hypocrites at best and criminals at worst.

Yet she had only met one Templar Knight in her life, and he was a good man. Sir Marcus de Rancourt had always done the right thing as far as she was concerned, and Thomas was quite taken with him. If all the Templars were like Marcus, then perhaps she was wrong about the Order itself, yet that was too simplistic. Sometimes, all it took was one bad apple, and she found it impossible to believe that all members of the Templar Order were good, though was willing to concede the majority might very well be. It still meant some within the Order could be behind whatever was happening, but what was it that was happening? She had no clue what it was that Chapon was involved in that had him so terrified he'd be willing to let Enzo have a go at him.

She finally turned to her enforcer. "Do you have any thoughts on this?"

His eyes flared slightly. "None worth mentioning, I'm sure."

She smiled gently at him. "You're not the fool you think you are, my friend. Out with it. What are you thinking?"

"I'm thinking that if Templars are involved, then we need a Templar to look into it."

Her smile spread. "I knew I didn't keep you around just for your good looks. We must send word to Sir Marcus immediately."

"How?"

"We'll have to send a messenger."

"The quickest would be the Templars themselves."

She shook her head. "No, we can't risk them reading it. If they are indeed behind this, we can't let them know we know. They wouldn't hesitate to kill us both."

He grunted. "They wouldn't find it so easy, ma'am."

She chuckled. "Even you, my friend, would have a difficult time, though I have no doubt you would take your fair share of them with you."

"Thank you, ma'am."

"We'll use a private messenger. It'll be a little slower, but safer." She grabbed a piece of paper and composed her message, beseeching help from someone she never would have imagined voluntarily inviting back into her life.

En Route to Paris, Kingdom of France

Marcus pursed his lips as they crested a rise, Paris revealed ahead. Isabelle visibly shivered.

"The last time I saw this place, it wasn't under the best of circumstances."

He frowned, agreeing with the young woman. "I remember it well, but as I said, that's not everyone, though it is a good reminder to be vigilant at all times." He urged his horse forward as the sun was low on the horizon, long shadows cast by anything above the ground. And by the time they reached the city, the light was dim, made dimmer so by the buildings that surrounded them.

Normally, he would lead them to the Templar Fortress, though not today. He had no business there, though would make certain to check in before he left. As was his duty. But for now, he was here to get the business of his journey concluded as quickly as possible. He navigated the now familiar streets leading to Thomas' family home, soon spotting it.

He pointed. "That's it."

Isabelle's eyes widened, her jaw dropping. "It's…"

"Not what you expected?"

Her shoulders slumped. "No, I suppose it isn't."

"Look around you, miss. Compare it not to what your imagination had led you to believe you would find, but compare it to reality."

Her jaw slowly shut as she stared at the poverty around them. "How do people live like this?"

"Quite happily. If they didn't, no one would."

As they neared the house, her expression softened slightly. "I suppose, compared to the others, it's in quite fine condition."

Marcus agreed. "Yes. Since Thomas found gainful employment, he's been doing many much-needed repairs, some of which resulted in the jealousy I was speaking of. These are poor people, but they're proud, most with good hearts. Treat them with respect, and they'll treat you with respect as well."

Those denizens he was referring to in the streets parted at the sight of a Templar Knight and his sergeant, though they didn't spare their glances at the young, beautiful woman accompanying two men sworn to celibacy. She smiled at her future neighbors, giving them a slight wave, though none returned it.

Marcus spotted the dull glow of a fire inside Thomas' home. "It would appear someone is here." He dismounted and tied up his horse, the others doing the same, then rapped on the door.

"Who is it?" The voice was deep, rough, and definitely not Thomas. Marcus gripped the hilt of his sword, Simon doing the same. Isabelle drew her newly acquired dagger and Marcus held out his free hand.

"Please put that away, miss, you're liable to stab yourself or one of us."

She frowned then tucked her knife back in her bag as he returned his attention to the task at hand.

"I am Sir Marcus de Rancourt of the Templar Order. I'm here to see Mr. Thomas Durant."

"Sir Marcus?" The man said it as if he recognized the name, and they heard heavy footfalls inside before the door was yanked open and they were greeted by a tree trunk. It was a sight that would have any lesser man soiling himself, and he wasn't certain how he'd have reacted if he didn't recognize the man as Thibault's enforcer Enzo. "How did you get here so quickly?"

Marcus' eyes narrowed. "What do you mean?"

Enzo stepped back and invited them inside. "I sent you a message this morning at Mrs. Thibault's request with respect to Thomas."

Marcus paused, glancing at Isabelle behind him, her greatest fear perhaps about to be proven true. "What about Thomas? He was supposed to return to the farm yesterday, but didn't arrive. We grew concerned. Did he not leave?"

"No. He—"

"That little imp!" cried Isabelle. "He *is* abandoning me!" She rushed inside, her head on a swivel as she searched for her betrayer.

"Excuse me, miss, you wouldn't be Isabelle, would you?"

She stopped and faced Enzo, her cheeks flush, her hands on her hips. "Yes, I would be. Why?"

Enzo smiled. "Thomas has spoken quite fondly of you."

"Oh? If he's so fond of me, then why is he abandoning our relationship in such a cowardly fashion?"

He stared at her, puzzled. "I'm not sure I understand."

"Well, that's why he hasn't returned, isn't it? He's leaving me!"

He shook his head. "No, miss, I'm afraid you don't understand. Thomas is missing. Nobody knows where he is."

Chapon Family Bakery
Paris, Kingdom of France

"There's something I need to tell you."

Chapon's wife stared at him, clearly having detected the nervousness in his voice. "What have you done now?"

He bristled slightly at the accusatory tone. "What makes you think I've done something?"

"Because I know that voice. Whenever you've done something idiotic, that's exactly how you sound."

He sighed. "We've been married too long. There's no keeping any secrets from you."

She eyed him. "Yet you have been keeping something from me, haven't you? You've changed the past couple of weeks. Something's wrong." She stared at his shaking hands then his bloodshot eyes. "You've been drinking, haven't you? You know how I feel about that!"

"No, I swear I haven't."

She huffed. "I know you go out at night. I'm not a fool. I feel you leave our bed. I hear you go out the front door thinking I won't because it's farther from our bed chambers. You don't think I hear you get back into our bed, barely before the sun rises, having just put the bread in the ovens. And look at you! You're a mess!" She jabbed a finger at him. "I want the truth, husband, all of the truth, and I want it now."

His shoulders sagged. She was right. She deserved the truth. This was the woman he loved, the woman he shared his life with, good and bad. She had stood beside him, shoulder to shoulder, as they went to Thibault in desperation to save their business. They had discussed their options beforehand, and settled upon the only one they had besides abandoning the business his grandfather had built. They had made sacrifices to repay the loan, their children had made sacrifices, and now he had put all that at risk. He had to tell her the truth, and all of it, not the partial less than honest version he had planned.

Yet he couldn't look her in the eye as he did.

"I've done something bad."

He could see her hands ringing in her lap. "What did you do?" There was no anger in her voice, only trepidation.

"It wasn't my fault. It was Henri's. He took me there the first time. I didn't want to go, because I knew how you'd feel about it, but he convinced me. He said he'd pay."

She said nothing, and it compelled him to continue speaking, each word out of his mouth a small relief.

"I went there the first time about a month ago. It's not far from here. Maybe ten minutes' walk. It's in a basement underneath that clothing shop you always stare at."

Her eyes flared. "The one I asked how it could possibly stay in business in this neighborhood?"

"Exactly, that's the one. Well, I found out how they stay in business."

"How?"

"Well, the clothing isn't really where they make their money. They make it in the basement."

"Doing what?"

66

"They sell something there. Something wonderful, but terrible at the same time."

"And just what is this wonderfully terrible thing?"

"It's something you inhale. It makes you feel fantastic. You forget all your problems, all your troubles, all your aches and pains. It allows you to escape reality, if only for a few hours."

"And Henri took you there?"

"Yes."

"And let me guess, you've gone back since?"

"Yes."

"How many times?"

"Too many to count. Almost every day for the past two weeks."

She inhaled quickly, struggling to control the anger he knew she was feeling. "And you pay money every time you go?"

"Yes."

"How much?"

"More than we can afford."

Her eyes widened then she glared at him. "Is that why Enzo was here? Have you not been paying down our loan?"

His eyes burned and his chest ached. "No. I'm ashamed to say I missed the last two payments."

She leaped to her feet and paced the room, her hands clenching and unclenching. "You realize that we put the business as collateral, don't you?"

"Yes, I know. That's why I'm so ashamed."

"Why did you let it happen? How could you do this?"

He closed his eyes, unable to look at the

67

disappointment on her face. "I couldn't help myself. I don't know. I don't know what happened to me. It's like I was drawn there every night. I would be lying in bed with you and I would just start to shake and hurt all over." He opened his eyes, pleading for understanding. "I needed it. I needed it and the more I got it, the more I needed it. I just don't understand why something that would make you feel so good, would hurt you so badly the next day, and make you crave it even more."

"Why are you telling me now?"

"Because…because we're in danger!" He sobbed, unable to control his emotions any longer.

She stared at him. "What do you mean?"

"I mean, Mrs. Thibault wanted to know why I had missed the payments."

"And you told her."

"I had to. I had no choice. Enzo was going to tear my arms off."

"Why would she threaten you like that? She knows that if you can't work, you can't pay her back."

"She doesn't care about the loan. In fact, she said she'd forgive the missed payments if I told her what she wanted to know."

His wife paused her pacing, regarding him as she processed this new piece of information. "She promised to forget the two payments you missed?"

"Yes."

Her draw dropped with renewed fear. "Oh my God! What have you done that she would agree to do this?"

He turned his back to her, the shame overwhelming. "Do you know Thomas Durant?"

"You know I know him. His mother and I were friends."

"Well, he followed me last night and they caught him."

A hand darted to her mouth. "And what are they going to do with him?"

"I don't know, but I fear they might kill him."

"And who are 'they?'"

He turned to face her. "It's the Templars."

Durant Residence
Paris, Kingdom of France

"What do you mean he's missing?"

Enzo sat in a chair at the lone table as Simon warmed his hands by the fire. Isabelle was clenching Marcus' arm, her entire body trembling. Enzo shrugged. "I mean, just that. He's missing. Since last night. Mrs. Thibault asked him to look into why some of our debtors have stopped paying—"

Marcus pursed his lips. "Why would she ask him to do that? Isn't that your job?"

Enzo shook his head. "No, she wanted somebody not quite so obvious to follow the baker, Mr. Chapon, to see where he was spending the money meant for his loan payments."

Isabelle gasped. "Why would he agree to that?"

Enzo seemed uncomfortable and looked away. "He did it for you, miss."

Tears welled in Isabelle's eyes. "What do you mean?"

"He came to Paris to ask if he could work for Mrs. Thibault only during the winter, so that he could spend the summer with you at the farm. She agreed, however had one condition, and that was to have him figure out why some of our debtors were no longer paying."

She buried her head in Marcus' chest. "It's all my fault!"

He patted her back. "No, it's not. And we don't even know what we're talking about yet." He returned

70

his attention to Enzo. "Tell me more about what happened yesterday."

"Thomas was supposed to follow the baker and see what he was up to. I assume he went to the bakery and waited outside to see if he left—"

"You assume?"

Enzo shrugged. "What else would he do? Anyway, this morning, when Thomas didn't show up, Mrs. Thibault grew concerned."

Isabelle sniffed. "I'm surprised that woman has any feelings whatsoever."

Enzo gave her a look that silenced her. "As I was saying, she grew concerned, so sent me to see if Mr. Chapon was at his bakery, or if he was still out, and Thomas was still possibly following him. I found Mr. Chapon at his bakery, so I knew something must have happened to Thomas. I told Mrs. Thibault, and she had me bring Mr. Chapon to meet with her. That's when we found out that indeed Thomas had followed him and had been caught by the people Mr. Chapon had been going to see."

"And just who are these people?"

Enzo frowned. "You wouldn't believe me if I told you. The baker was quite convinced that not only was his life in danger, but so was that of Thomas, and after I heard who was involved, I became convinced that he might be right."

Marcus tensed. "Who are they?"

Enzo shifted in his chair. "According to Mr. Chapon, it's you."

Marcus' eyebrows shot up and Simon spun away from the fire. "What do you mean, him?"

Enzo shook his head. "No, I don't mean *him*. I mean

you, as in Templars."

Chapon Family Bakery
Paris, Kingdom of France

Chapon bolted upright, his entire body covered in sweat, the bedding he lay upon soaked. His body trembled, every muscle contracted, the pounding in his head unbearable. How he had fallen asleep at all was beyond him.

"Someone's at the door."

It was only then that he realized his wife was also sitting up, her ear cocked. Somebody pounded on the door again.

"Who could it be at such an hour?"

He frowned. "Nobody good, I'm certain, but if we don't answer it, they'll wake the entire neighborhood."

"What if it's those Templars?"

"It's probably just some drunk. It wouldn't be the first time one came here looking for food."

She lit a candle, revealing her frown. "It's probably Henri."

He shook his head. "No, I don't think so, he knows better." Whoever it was, pounded again. He stood, his mental and physical torture momentarily forgotten, replaced with concern for his family as his children took notice on the other side of the wall. His wife clutched his arm and followed him through the bedroom door. "No, you stay here."

"I'm not letting you go out there alone."

He eyed her. "And just what do you think you could do against Templars?"

"I could raise Holy hell, that's what I could do. The entire neighborhood will be awake before they could silence me."

He smiled and wrapped an arm around her, squeezing her tightly against him. Together, they headed for the door at the rear of their home and opened it to find a sight far more terrifying than a dozen Templar Knights.

It was Enzo.

"What do you want at this time of night?" snapped his wife, much to his horror and Enzo's surprise.

"I have friends who would speak with you."

He wasn't sure what to make of the claim the man had a friend, let alone friends. "Who?"

Enzo beckoned him to step forward and he did. The beast of a man pointed toward the end of the alleyway and Chapon turned to look, then nearly soiled himself at the sight of a Templar Knight and his sergeant, both on horseback.

His wife gasped. "Oh no!" She reached to pull him back inside, but he resisted. If these men wanted him, no flimsy wooden door would hold them back.

"Why? Why are they here?" His eyes narrowed. "And why are they with you?"

"These are friends."

He grew faint. "Friends? Did you make some sort of deal with them?"

Enzo shook his head. "No, I mean they're *friends*. They're friends of Thomas."

Relief swept over Chapon as he realized exactly who these men were, though if the Templars were indeed behind what he had become involved in, these men could be as well. "What do they want with me?"

"They want to ask you about Thomas. They want to find him."

He frowned. "Well, I don't know where he is."

"But you know where he was last seen."

He lowered his voice. "But I can't tell them that. If I do, then it could mean the death of us."

Enzo leaned closer. "Trust me, I know you fear me, but I'm nothing compared to the wrath that Sir Marcus will bring down on you if anything happens to his friend."

Urine flowed freely down Chapon's leg once again.

Durant Residence
Paris, Kingdom of France

Isabelle placed the crossbar over the door, locking herself inside, though she was well aware if anyone were determined to get in, the flimsy construction of this home would never keep them out. She set about lighting every candle and lamp she could find, and stoked the fire to remove the chill and the darkness from the unfamiliar building that was the family home of the man she loved, and now knew hadn't abandoned her.

She was racked with guilt over her previous thoughts. How could she have ever doubted his love? How could she have ever thought the worst of him? How could she have ever said those horrible things about him? She had been so wrong. She didn't deserve the love of a man such as him. He was the best person she had ever met, the most unusual person she had ever met. She had grown up in a farming village. Everyone toiled day in and day out on their farms. All the boys she knew, all the boys she had grown up with—and those were few—remained farmers. They were good people, but they weren't interesting to her.

Perhaps that's why she had always been infatuated with those from far away. Most of her youth had been spent fantasizing about Marcus every day, the tales her friend, his late sister, told of him fascinating. She had loved him for as long as she could remember, and when she finally met him, had been broken-hearted at the fact he hadn't returned her love the moment they met. It had been a confusing time, for she had built up this fantasy that they were already husband and wife, and had just been living apart while he heroically defended the Christian pilgrims in the Holy Land from the Muslim hordes who would do them harm.

But he had crushed her with his rejection, though he had been as gentle as he could be about it. The man was a monk sworn to celibacy, after all, and had no experience with women, nor did he intend to gain any. She had been a young fool, but when Thomas had been brought to the farm by Marcus and his men, she had a new person to focus her attention on, someone more her age, someone actually available, someone who hadn't taken a vow of celibacy.

Someone willing to love her back.

And yet in some ways, he was simply another Marcus, someone she had nothing in common with, someone from far away. Yes, she truly did love him. She recognized now that her feelings toward Marcus were merely a childhood infatuation and that it wasn't real love. With Thomas, it was pure, and she had been terrible toward him this past day. Now she was horribly worried for him, and prayed that Marcus and Simon saved him.

With every source of light now blazing, she took a moment to examine her surroundings. It was similar to her own home, though there were few personal touches. Thomas' mother had died some time ago, and he had grown up quite poor, so perhaps it wasn't surprising that a widower and his son didn't go to the effort to make a house feel like a home.

We'll have to change that when we're married.

She explored the rest of the home, then smiled at

the sight of Thomas' bed. She looked about the room to make sure she was indeed alone, then climbed into it, hugging the beddings and breathing in his essence, then quickly scrambled out, remembering that Enzo was probably the last to have slept there. She brushed off whatever remnants of Enzo she might have picked up, then smiled.

I can't wait until we're married.

Her smile spread as she remembered what Enzo had said. Thibault had agreed to their plan, and that meant there was nothing that could stop them now. They would be married. They would split their time between Paris and Crécy-la-Chapelle, and they would be blissfully happy, filling both homes with children and laughter.

She dropped onto the bed, overwhelmed with the sadness reality brought with it. None of her dreams could come true if Thomas were dead, and at this very moment, she had no idea if the love of her life, if the key to her future happiness, was alive.

78

Chapon Family Bakery
Paris, Kingdom of France

Marcus regarded the terrified baker sitting across from him. Simon stood in one corner as intimidating as ever, with Enzo opposite him equally so. Chapon's wife sat beside her husband, holding his hand. With the poor woman as scared as her husband, Marcus went with the gentle approach, as he was quite certain these were good people innocently mixed up in something beyond their experience.

He smiled. "Now, tell me everything you know, and don't leave out any detail. It may be critical."

Chapon shifted in his chair. "I don't know where to begin."

His wife slapped his arm. "At the beginning, you fool. With Henri."

"Oh, right. Well, Henri told me about this place that he started going to."

"Where?"

"Where you could inhale something that made you feel really good. Where you can forget all your troubles. I didn't want to go because I knew my wife wouldn't approve of anything such as this, but Henri spoke so enthusiastically of it, and I was so miserable with our financial situation, that I decided to go since Henri offered to pay for me the first time. I figured it couldn't hurt anyone just to try it and see what he was talking about, and it would at least shut him up."

"And who is Henri to you?"

79

"Just a friend that I grew up with."

"And what does he do?"

"He's a fishmonger."

"Does he have any connection with the Templars?"

Chapon shook his head. "Not that I'm aware of. Perhaps he supplies them with fish, though if he had a contract like that, I would think his situation would be much better than it is."

"So, you went to this place with Henri to try this thing that you inhaled. What happened then?"

"I tried it, and I suppose I enjoyed it a little too much. I found after a few days that I was craving it or at least something."

"So, you went back?"

"Yes."

"Did you go back with Henri?"

"No, I went by myself."

"And they had no problem with you doing that?"

"No. In fact, they were quite inviting, very happy to see me."

"How many times have you been back?"

"Many. In fact, tonight is the first night I haven't been there in two weeks."

Marcus frowned. "And last night was when they captured Thomas."

"Yes."

"And you obviously saw this take place."

"No, I didn't know. I mean, not until after they brought him in. They somehow knew he was following me."

"If they're well organized like I've seen in the Holy Land, they were probably watching you. I've seen

80

where they pay children to keep an eye out for anything unusual. I wouldn't be surprised, with you being a regular customer, if they didn't have someone watching your bakery. A lookout likely spotted Thomas, and that was all it would take."

Chapon's head bobbed. "It was a young boy who reported Thomas to the men who run the place."

Marcus chewed his cheek for a moment. "My concern is that you not showing up there tonight breaks the pattern you've set for two weeks. They obviously told you not to tell anyone what had happened last night, and of course, if they had someone watching you yesterday, they absolutely would have had someone watching you today. And Enzo would have been seen escorting you to meet with Mrs. Thibault. If you don't show up tonight, they'll assume you told her about them."

"What should I do?"

"You should go," said Simon from the corner of the room. "If you don't, they might hurt Thomas."

Marcus disagreed. "No, I'm not sure that's the wisest of moves. If they have someone watching the bakery, then they will have seen us arrive. If he goes now, they'll know something's wrong."

"Then what should we do?" asked Mrs. Chapon.

"Our first priority is to save Thomas, but his life will continue to be in danger as long as these people are in business."

"What about us?" cried Chapon. "What about my family? I have children. Who's going to protect us?"

"We will. We'll take you to the Fortress. You'll be safe there."

Chapon's eyes bulged. "Are you insane? It's

81

Templars who are behind this. While I might trust you and your sergeant, I certainly don't trust your order. If it is Templars behind this, then whoever's in charge most likely lives within those walls."

Marcus shook his head. "Though we are an order of monks, and evil can always penetrate where goodness thrives, I simply cannot believe that my brothers are involved. If they are, I'm quite certain it isn't sanctioned."

"That may be, but there's no way I'm taking my family into what may be a den of wolves."

He understood the man's concern, though only if members of his order were indeed involved, and he still hadn't heard any evidence of that. "What makes you say that it's Templars? Did you see any of my brothers there?"

"No."

"Then why do you think it's Templars?"

"It's Templars who are bringing them the product."

Marcus exchanged a surprised look with Simon. "What do you mean? What is this product? You said you inhale it. What is it?"

"They call it opium. I've seen them open the packages. It arrives as a black paste, and then they do something with it and put it in a clay pot they have over a lamp. They bring it to a boil then attach a pipe to it. You put your mouth around the end of the pipe and breathe it in. After a few minutes, it's as if you're floating in the clouds, and a euphoria sweeps over you. You're in ecstasy. It's really hard to describe. It's unlike anything I've ever felt before. It's the most incredible feeling I've ever had in my life."

Marcus frowned. He had heard of opium during his

time in the Holy Land, and nothing of what he heard was good. And until now, he hadn't realized it had made it this deep into Europe. "How long do its effects last?"

"As long as you can afford to keep giving them money. I've seen people in there that I swear haven't left in days. They have people that go around and give them food and water. I've even seen them cleaning them up, giving them fresh clothing."

"And they said that the Templars bring them the product? How?"

"I overheard one of them talking to another. It comes from somewhere far away, someplace I've never heard of. Persia, I think they said. It's transported in your caravans."

"I'll need you to show me where this place is."

Chapon's shoulders slumped and he sighed. "Very well. But you said you would protect me and my family. How?"

"Enzo will take your wife and children to Thomas Durant's house, and he'll stand guard until we get back. You know where he lives?"

"Yes."

"Good. You'll show us to this den of iniquity, then you'll go immediately back to Thomas' house."

Chapon squeezed his wife's hand, relief on his face. "Very well. Thank you."

Unknown Location

Thomas lifted his head, his world a haze of confusion and lethargy. What had first been exquisite ecstasy had eventually become sickening. He wasn't sure what time it was, though he did recollect natural light at one point, and now it was dark again. He assumed he had been here for at least a day. They had shoved a pipe in his mouth and forced him to breathe it in. He had struggled against them as best he could, but it was useless, and after a few moments, when its effect took hold, he had willingly inhaled the vile substance, for it had to be vile. Anything that could make one feel so good had to be sinful. The feeling was indescribable. He had heard others talk of what sex felt like, and he imagined it was much like this, though this had to be better—sex couldn't last an entire day. And he suspected that perhaps if it could, it too would no longer feel as good by the end of it.

He had backed off inhaling from the pipe, still keeping it in his mouth in case anyone was watching, and whenever they approached to check on him as they did the other dozen souls that lay about on comfortable cushions in the room they had moved him into, he was compelled to draw on the pipe, causing the water to gurgle, satisfying his keepers.

He struggled to pierce the fog in his brain. It was as if there were a stone barrier between him and the mind he knew lay beyond. At this very moment, he was the most aware he had been since last night, and heard the rapid-fire coded knock at the door at the top of a set of stairs to his left, a sense of urgency suggested in the speed. The door was opened and somebody stepped inside. He couldn't make out who it was in the dim light, but the voice was unmistakably that of a child.

"I have to see the master."

"Why?"

"I have news of the baker."

Whoever the master was, he was within earshot. "What news do you have, boy?"

He recognized the voice as the man who had interrogated him last night.

The boy rushed down the stairs. "Templars, sir. Templars came to the bakery with the beast."

"When?"

"Just now. As soon as I saw them go inside, I ran here as fast as I could."

"Very well. Pay the boy." A coin was pushed into the boy's hand. "And don't come back here."

"Yes, sir." The boy scurried up the stairs and was out the door moments later as he carried out his final instruction. The man in charge slapped his hands together.

"Get everybody out of here. We're moving. Grab the pipes, lamps, and bowls. I don't want to have to replace them."

"And the bedding?" asked someone.

"No time."

Groans of complaint from those around him had a faint surge of hope rush through him at the idea his ordeal might be about to finish.

"Get them all out of here!" ordered the man in charge, the several people in his employ hauling those around him to their feet and pushing them up the stairs.

"What about him?" asked a man now standing in front of him.

"Take him with us."

Thomas slumped on his cushions, all hope drained from him.

De Rancourt Family Farm
Crécy-la-Chapelle, Kingdom of France

"Who goes there?"

David bolted upright in bed at the shrill sound of Lady Joanne's chambermaid, Beatrice, as she repeated her demand amid the barking of Tanya.

"Who goes there, I said!"

David jumped from his bed and grabbed his bow along with a quiver of arrows, slinging it over his shoulder as he kicked Jeremy's bunk. "Get up! Something's going on."

Jeremy groaned but didn't move.

"Get up! There's trouble!"

Jeremy leaped from the bed as David charged through the doors of their barracks and down the hill. It was dark, the only light from a quarter moon and the stars, but he could still make out that the door to the farmhouse was open.

"I have a message for Sir Marcus," a voice called from the dark, accompanied by the whinny of a horse.

"Stay where you are, or I'll unleash the hound!"

They both reached the house and took up position in front of Beatrice, the string on their bows drawn taut, arrows at the ready.

"Advance and be recognized!" ordered David.

A horse and rider slowly approached, the shadowy figure becoming clear, his hands raised high.

"That's close enough. Who are you?"

"I'm a messenger from Paris. I have an urgent

message for Sir Marcus de Rancourt, Templar Knight."

David relaxed slightly. "Are you a Templar?"

"No, I'm a private messenger."

"Who sent you?"

"A Mrs. Thibault contracted my services."

David tensed. If Thibault was contacting Marcus, then something had definitely happened to Thomas, and Isabelle's fears of having been abandoned were a false hope. "Dismount and bring us the message, but keep your hands where we can see them."

The man complied and he cautiously approached, a message gripped in his hand, high above his head. Tanya growled and Jeremy lowered his bow, taking the message. Lady Joanne stepped forward.

"Let me see that." Jeremy handed her the folded paper and she turned to Beatrice. "Stoke the fire and light the lamps."

"Yes, ma'am." Beatrice disappeared inside, and in short order a dull glow turned into enough light to read by. David turned to Jeremy.

"Watch him."

Jeremy pulled a little tighter on his bowstring.

"If he moves—"

"It'll be the last thing he does."

David went inside and found Joanne reading the message, her eyes bulging. "What does it say?"

"It's from Mrs. Thibault to Sir Marcus. She says that Thomas is missing, and that the last person to see him alive said it was Templars that had taken him."

David gasped. "That can't possibly be."

She shook the page. "Yet that's what it says. She's asking Sir Marcus to come and help find Thomas."

"But he's already there."

"Yes, but for this message to arrive by tonight means it had been sent before he could have possibly got there. The messenger may have very well passed them on the road to Paris."

David's mind raced with the implications. "I have to go there."

"Why?"

"Because if Templars did indeed take Thomas, and it wasn't a simple misunderstanding, then something has gone wrong and they'll require people they can trust." He looked at Lady Joanne and Beatrice, then at the children whose heads were now poking around the corner. He frowned. "But I can't leave you alone."

Lady Joanne batted a hand at him. "Pish! Don't worry about us. We can take care of ourselves. Besides, we're surrounded by friends here, and nothing happens here regardless."

David's eyebrows rose slightly. "That hasn't been my experience." He eyed the mastiff still in the doorway. "I'll leave the dog with you."

Joanne shook her head. "No, take the beast with you. She's too much trouble when her master isn't here. Besides, you're always speaking of how good she is in a fight. I fear you may need her more than we will."

Outside the Clothing Shop
Paris, Kingdom of France

"That's it there."

Marcus looked across the street at where Chapon was pointing. The building was a rather nondescript shop like any other closed for the night, nothing suggesting anything untoward was happening inside. "And you said it's in the basement?"

"Yes. In the alleyway there's a door on the side. It's a coded knock. Three knocks, then one, then two. They'll open the Judas door, and if they recognize you, they let you in."

"And if they don't?"

Chapon shrugged. "I don't know. I assume it can't be good."

Marcus grunted. "No, I suppose it wouldn't be." He turned to Chapon. "Go back to Thomas' house now. Don't stop anywhere. Don't talk to anyone."

"Yes, sir. Good luck." Chapon hurried away, soon lost in the dark Paris night.

"What do you want to do?" asked Simon.

"I think we may be too late."

"What makes you say that?"

"Look." Marcus pointed across the street at two men, lying on the periphery of the street, more passed out farther down the road. "Those look like customers."

Simon cursed. "You're right. They must have found out we were coming, so they kicked everyone out and shut down their operation." He eyed the abandoned men. "Do you think one of them is Thomas?"

"No, but if we don't find him inside, we'll check these ones just in case." Marcus drew his sword and advanced across the street, Simon doing the same, both their heads on swivels as they watched for any hostiles that might be lurking in the shadows. Marcus stopped in front of the door and knocked three times, then once, then twice, and the Judas hole remained closed.

He pushed on the door and it swung open, a powerful stench wafting out. He stepped inside and cursed at what was clearly an abandoned operation. "It looks like they left this place in a hurry." He descended the stairs, followed by Simon, and slowly advanced into the room, sword at the ready, making certain they were alone.

Simon kicked at a cushion. "They definitely knew we were coming."

Marcus frowned. "I'm beginning to think we should have accompanied Mr. Chapon back to Thomas' house, rather than let him go alone."

"You think someone might try to hurt him?"

"If you had just been forced to close down your highly profitable enterprise because of the loose lips of one of your customers, what would you do?"

Simon shrugged. "I know what I'd do, but I'm a bastard. Though why close down? Is there anything criminal about what's going on here? Is using opium a crime?"

"No, it isn't. At least not that I'm aware of, though it is a sin. If everyone is aware of what you're doing, then your customers go away because they don't want to be revealed as the sinners they are."

Simon's head bobbed slowly. "Makes sense."

"The baker went to great lengths to hide what he was up to, and look where it got him. I'm sure the others who are in here are in similar situations. If the neighbors knew what was going on, they would likely put a swift end to it, so secrecy would be of utmost importance." Marcus picked through the remains of the abandoned operation, finding little of consequence until his candle sputtered and he bent over to pick up another one. "Now, this is interesting."

"What?"

Marcus picked up an ornate cushion, a coat of arms carefully embroidered on one side. "This looks familiar."

Simon stepped over and examined the cushion. "Sorry, it looks like any other coat of arms to me."

"Yes. But what is it doing here? I've seen this before, but what is any coat of arms doing here in a place such as this?"

"Could they have stolen it?"

"I find that difficult to believe." Marcus pointed at the other cushions near the one he had found in the corner of the room. "Look how this particular area is set up, and that one over there." He pointed to the opposite corner. "Much finer than these other stations, and they have privacy screens. I'm willing to bet these are for their higher-end clientele."

Simon's eyebrows rose slightly. "You believe nobility is coming here?"

"Possibly."

"Well, that changes things, doesn't it?"

Marcus sighed. "If nobility is indeed involved, then they will do whatever it takes to keep that fact a secret.

"Which means they won't hesitate to kill Thomas if they feel he's a threat."

"Exactly. Let's get home. As much as I believe Enzo could take on a small army, I think it's best we're there to protect the women and children." He handed the embroidered cushion to Simon. "Take this with us. I need to show it to somebody tomorrow."

En Route to Durant Residence
Paris, Kingdom of France

Chapon rushed back toward Thomas' home, his heart fluttering at every sound, every shuffle in the darkness. Good people weren't out at this hour, though at the moment, he didn't feel like good people. He was a sinner of the worst kind. No, he hadn't killed anyone— he had done something far worse—he had betrayed his wife, his family. He had risked all their futures merely for his own pleasure. Yet was it his fault? He had become dependent on this vile opium from its very first use. He craved the sensations that it brought him, then dreaded the horrors it left behind. And despite the knowledge of what was to come, and what had been, he would give everything he had for one more draw on the pipe that had brought so much grief.

Thomas' home wasn't far now, only a few more minutes. He had been there before, years ago, in happier times when Thomas was a young boy and his parents were very much alive. The boy's father wasn't exactly a good man. It was well known that he was a forger of some skill, though he had never hurt anyone directly that he was aware of, and he loved his family as any good man would. He was merely doing whatever it took to keep them clothed and fed, and if the roles were reversed, Chapon couldn't say he wouldn't have done the same thing if his skills matched that of the elder Durant.

He barely knew Thomas, though he knew him enough to be racked with guilt over what might have happened to him. He prayed that Thomas was safe and that the Templars had already rescued him, though he feared the worst. If Thomas were dead because he had followed him, because he hadn't paid his debt, he would never forgive himself.

"Going somewhere?"

Chapon resisted the instinct to stop walking and continued, not responding to the voice behind him.

"Stop, or I'll gut your wife and children."

He froze, every muscle in his body tensing.

"Turn and face me."

He slowly turned to see a shadowy figure standing there, moonlight glinting off a drawn dagger.

"You were told not to tell anyone."

He gulped. "I'm sorry. I had no choice."

"One always has choices." The man lunged at him and Chapon dove to the side, rolling on the hard ground. The blade nicked his upper arm and he winced. He scrambled to his feet as the man descended upon him. A horse's whinny was followed by hooves galloping toward them. His attacker spun at the sound and Chapon took advantage. He sprinted as fast as he could away from the man, stumbling each time he turned his head to see if he was being pursued, the inky blackness making it difficult. He could hear nothing over his own footfalls and gasping breaths, and much to his relief, he spotted the door of Thomas' house ahead, the dull glow of a fire and lamps inside signaling sanctuary.

He reached the door and hammered on it. "It's me! Let me in!"

The door opened revealing Enzo, the most beautiful sight he had seen all day. He rushed past him and into the home of a boy he might have condemned to death. "Close the door! Close the door!"

Enzo, to his horror, stepped outside, looking in all directions before finally answering his plea.

"What's wrong, my dear?" asked his wife, rushing toward him, her eyes wide.

He grabbed her and the children, hugging them hard as tears flowed freely down his cheeks. "They almost caught me."

"Who, Daddy?" asked his daughter.

He suddenly remembered where he was and who he was with, and the fact that his children, he hoped, remained blissfully unaware of what exactly was going on. "Nothing. Don't worry about it." He patted his daughter on her head. "Shouldn't you two be asleep?"

"They refused to go down until you arrived."

"Well, I've arrived, so to bed with you."

His wife disappeared with the children, coming back a few minutes later as he warmed by the fire. Enzo sat in a chair positioned by the door, ready to take on all comers, and the man he once feared now brought him immeasurable comfort.

"You're bleeding."

"Huh?"

His wife pointed at his arm, concern growing on her face. "You're bleeding!"

He looked, the wound having been forgotten, and the sight of the sleeve of his jacket soaked in blood had him grow faint, the world spinning as he collapsed on the floor.

En Route to Durant Residence
Paris, Kingdom of France

"I didn't see anything that suggested our order was involved."

Marcus agreed with his sergeant's observance. "Nor would I have expected to. If Templars are indeed involved, it sounded to me as if they are merely transporting the goods from wherever they're getting it to here."

"Could it be as simple as that? Perhaps they don't know what they're transporting. I know I wouldn't recognize opium if I saw it. Until this very evening, I had no idea it was a black paste."

"My understanding is it comes in different forms." Marcus exhaled loudly, his breath fogging in front of him. "I hope you're right. I would hate to think anyone in our order could be so vile as to distribute something such as this that causes so much harm. We have to determine the truth and rescue Thomas. If our brothers are involved, I don't want to risk them finding out we are pursuing them."

"I fail to see how we're going to find the boy now that they've disappeared."

Marcus nodded toward the cushion Simon held. "I have a thought about that. What you're holding may be the key." He dismounted from his horse and tied it up in front of Thomas' home. He knocked on the door.

"Who is it?" boomed Enzo from the other side.

"It's Sir Marcus and Simon."

Enzo opened the door and they stepped inside, the massive man making a point of looking out at the street.

"Is something wrong?"

"Something happened. Mr. Chapon was attacked on his way back."

Marcus cursed and saw Chapon at the table, his wife dabbing at a cut on his arm. "Simon, take a look at that." His sergeant, trained as all Templars were in treating battlefield wounds, sprang into action. Marcus turned back to Enzo. "Who did it?"

Thibault's enforcer returned to a chair by the door. "He doesn't know. It was too dark. But it was someone involved with the opium."

"He's lucky to have gotten away, and we were wise to have brought his family here. We'll remain here tonight, but before tomorrow is through, we'll have to find some place safer, though for the moment, the only place I can think of is the Templar Fortress." He stared at the cushion Simon had tossed aside and smiled. "Though perhaps there is another place."

En Route to Paris, Kingdom of France

David peered into the darkness ahead, barely seeing the road they were on. Instead of relying on his own senses, he gave the horse her head, keeping a light hold on the reins, letting the magnificent creature he now rode use her superior eyesight to guide them safely toward Paris. While their pace was slower than the gallop they would be traveling at in the light of day, they would still arrive by morning, and hopefully in time to help Marcus.

Tanya ran by their side, her tongue hanging out of her mouth, all indications she was as happy as could be, occasionally racing off to chase some random animal that happened to capture her attention. He never worried about her. She would always catch up, and if she didn't, she had proven in the past she knew her way home.

"Do you really think Templars are involved?" asked Jeremy.

David shook his head. "I can't see it, though I don't know what it is they're supposed to be involved in. My guess is it's simply a misunderstanding. Thibault is the worst sort, so if she had a run-in with our order, it's quite likely they're on the side of right. If they do indeed have Thomas, then I'm quite certain he is perfectly safe, and word of that fact has probably already been sent to the farm and will arrive tomorrow."

"I hope you're right, though if that were indeed true, and it was merely a dispute between our order and Mrs. Thibault, I can't believe she would send a letter. She's not the sort."

David chewed his cheek, troubled by Jeremy's assessment of the situation, for he was right. Thibault had never shown that she had much of a compassionate side, and if she were in a dispute with his order, she was likely in the wrong, so she would never bring attention to herself. She would know that Thomas was safe with the Templars, and he would get word to Marcus if he indeed needed help. A pit formed in his stomach. "I fear you might be right." He was about to urge the horse on a little faster, then stopped himself. If his mare broke a leg in the dark, any gain in time would be lost ten-fold.

He just had to have faith that Marcus already knew something was wrong, and was taking action with Simon. And if all went well, by the time they arrived in the morning, they would find Thomas safe and happy with Isabelle.

Durant Residence
Paris, Kingdom of France

Marcus woke to a fabulous aroma, somebody in the next room cooking up a feast to start their day. He rose from his corner of the room, having slept on the floor all night except for his two-hour shift standing watch. He stretched out the cramps that sleeping on a hard surface always brought, smiling at the cheerful conversation taking place between Isabelle and Mrs. Chapon. He checked his clothes then stepped into the main living area to find Enzo, Simon, and the Chapon family already eating, and cursed himself for being the tardy one.

"I wouldn't have thought you'd be the last one to rise," commented Mrs. Chapon.

He smiled sheepishly. "I guess I was more tired than I realized. I apologize."

"No need to apologize. Just find yourself a seat and I'll get you a plate."

Simon rose from his chair, shoveling the last of his food into his mouth. "Here. Take mine. I'm done."

Marcus sat and a plate was put in front of him, as hearty a meal as he had ever experienced on the farm. "Where did this come from? I can't imagine that Thomas kept this place well stocked with food."

"Enzo went out and got us what we needed."

"I see. Let's limit our trips outside. We need to keep a low profile. Enzo, you can go out if absolutely necessary, since the neighbors already know you've been staying here, but no mention can be made of Mr. Chapon and his family."

"Yes, sir."

Simon warmed his hands by the fire. "So, what is our plan today?"

Marcus swallowed. "I think we're going to drop in on an old friend."

Simon cocked an eyebrow. "We have friends?"

"Sir Denys de Montfort. He should be able to tell us whose coat of arms is embroidered on that cushion."

"And knowing that will accomplish what?"

"It gives us a lead. If the owner of that cushion was set up there in such a fashion as to have a corner reserved for himself, he's clearly a frequent customer who pays a premium. If they've set up shop somewhere else, they'll be certain to let him know where. We might be able to follow him and find Thomas."

"I hadn't thought of that. That's good thinking, that is."

"I have my moments."

"Does that fine, noble-bred brain of yours tell you how we can protect these good people, perhaps by taking advantage of our friend?"

Marcus chuckled again. "Yes, it had occurred to me, however I didn't want to be presumptuous and bring them with us. We'll ask Sir Denys if he wouldn't mind taking them under his protection, and if he agrees, we'll escort them there ourselves."

Chapon put his fork down. "Who is this Sir Denys you speak of?"

"A man who has helped us in the past."

"And you trust him with the lives of my wife and

102

children?"

"I trust him with the life of Isabelle, which should tell you all you need to know."

Isabelle stepped over to the table to reassure Chapon. "Lady Joanne has told me what happened, and I do believe we can trust Sir Denys."

"He has a substantial personal guard as he's a member of the King's Court," added Marcus. "You'll be safe there, and no one will think to look for you there either."

"And should they follow us?" asked Simon.

"We will have to take precautions that they don't. I just wish we had more men."

A knock at the door had them all spinning toward the sound.

"Should we answer?" whispered Isabelle, her eyes wide with fear.

Marcus indicated for Mrs. Chapon to take the children to the back room then nodded at Enzo, standing by the door. "Go ahead."

"Who is it?" rumbled the man in his most annoyed voice yet.

"It is David and Jeremy, squires of Sir Marcus de Rancourt."

Marcus smiled, saying a silent prayer to the Good Lord who had delivered him the men he needed. "Let them in, let them in!"

Enzo opened the door and David and Jeremy tentatively entered, Tanya rushing into the house, making a beeline directly for her master. Marcus gave her a hug and scratch, his squires both smiling broadly as they spotted their comrades. Enzo closed the door

103

behind them after checking outside.

"I'd chastise you for being here, however your timing is fortuitous. I must ask, however, why *are* you here?"

David looked at the strangers in the room. "Is it safe to speak in present company?"

"Yes. There are no secrets here."

"Very well. We received an urgent message from Mrs. Thibault addressed to you, indicating Thomas was missing and that Templars were involved. It arrived last evening, and we left immediately. Is it true? Has something happened to Thomas?"

"Yes. He's been kidnapped. It has something to do with opium. It would appear some in our order are using our caravans to transport it into the city." He indicated the baker. "This man, Mr. Chapon, was one of their customers who became dependent upon the substance and neglected his debt payments to Mrs. Thibault. She asked Thomas to follow him to see where he was spending his money, and unfortunately, Thomas was caught in the process."

"Is he…" Jeremy paused, glancing at Isabelle. "Is he…are we sure he's alive?"

"We're operating under the assumption he is. They moved their place of operations, and when we searched it last night, there was no evidence of anybody having been killed."

"But why would they be keeping him alive? What purpose would it serve?" David punched Jeremy, heading off any more awkward questions that might panic Isabelle.

"I'm not certain." Marcus turned to Chapon. "Would they know of me?"

"What do you mean?"

"Would they know that Thomas has Templars as friends?"

"Oh, everybody knows that." He cast his eyes at his plate. "In fact, I might have made mention of it after his capture."

"Then that might be why. If Templars aren't operating this enterprise and are merely the suppliers, then likely none of our order were there. So, they would be reticent to kill Thomas without first making certain they weren't killing a friend of their suppliers."

Simon grunted. "Then we don't have much time, do we?"

"No. If their suppliers are in Paris, then they might already be making inquiries. Thomas may only have hours to live."

"Then it is important we make haste."

Marcus gestured toward his squires. "Feed yourselves, then help me into my armor. It's in quite a state after Simon removed it last night."

Simon grunted. "I can't remember the last time I had to remove your armor. I'm out of practice."

David, the senior among the two, pointed at Jeremy. "See to Sir Marcus' armor. I'll eat first then you'll eat while I dress him."

Marcus pointed toward the next room and Jeremy disappeared inside, muttered curses erupting at Marcus' apparently accurate assessment of the state of his equipment.

Simon grinned. "I bet you won't ask me to remove your armor again, will you?"

De Montfort Estate
Paris, Kingdom of France

Sir Denys de Montfort leaned back, exhaling blissfully. It was a wondrous thing his friend had introduced him to. He could never have imagined that sensations such as these were possible. He had been drunk many a time in his day, many a time in the past month, and when balanced correctly, tremendous enjoyment could be had indulging in the various alcoholic beverages available to men with means.

But nothing compared to this.

He had heard tell of this opium, though had never seen nor met anyone who had experienced it in person. Men who had fought in the Holy Land spoke of it, but none among his circle of nobility. But an overheard conversation whispered in the corridors of the Palace had him posing questions. Apparently, the black paste had finally made it to Paris, and the person who had discovered the fact was extolling its virtues to several of the more junior members of the Court. He had insisted they bring him along on their first outing, the entire notion sounding entertaining.

It had been a hole of a place, and he had only gone the once. Yet once was enough for him to want it more, for the effects were far more pleasurable than alcohol could ever hope to be. Arrangements had been made, an exorbitant sum paid for a bowl, pipe, lamp, and a supply for several sessions, a supply that had only arrived two nights before.

This was only his third time partaking of this

newfound pleasure, yet he knew it was but one of many more. He had to tell his friends of this, though he was uncertain whom he could trust. This was clearly a sinful practice, made even more so by the fact its proprietors appeared to be running their entire operation out of the basement of a building that lay in the slums of the capital.

And that fact presented an opportunity.

If he played his cards right, he could set up his own operation in a more upscale facility where his friends and colleagues could partake, not in squalor but in opulence.

A knock at his bedchamber door would normally have surprised him, but in his relaxed state, his head merely lolled to the side. "Yes?"

"Sir, I'm sorry to disturb you, but you have guests."

He cursed, staring at the pipe and bowl, the sweet opium inside, heated by a lamp underneath. He had only inhaled a handful of times so far, and most of his faculties were still with him. However, entertaining guests might not be wise. In fact, having partaken at this early hour hadn't been the wisest of moves. Why he had done so, he wasn't certain. In fact, it was foolish, for he was due in court in mere hours.

It was your hands.

He stared at them. What had once been a bundle of jitters, were now steady. He wasn't sure why they had been shaking, but for some reason, he knew the opium would steady them. It had to be nerves, though he couldn't imagine for the life of him about what he might be nervous. When he recalled that he hadn't a care in the world when he partook of the opium, he thought it a logical remedy.

"Tell them I'm not receiving at the moment."

"I shall, sir, however it is Sir Marcus de Rancourt and his sergeant, Simon Chastain."

A smile spread at their names. "Have them brought to the sitting room. I'll be there momentarily."

"Right away, sir."

He heard his manservant retreat from the door. He rose from his chair positioned near the fire and extinguished the opium lamp. He quickly donned some clothes that would normally have been put on for him, then rushed out the door and down the stairs, smiling broadly at the sight of two men he considered friends, two men who had saved his life only months before.

Marcus and his trusted companion Simon.

"What a delight to see you! To what do I owe the privilege?"

His guests bowed and Denys waved them off. "No need for formalities here, gentlemen, we are friends, are we not?"

Marcus smiled. "I would be honored to be considered your friend, sir."

Denys decided to have a little fun with the gruff sergeant. "And you, Sergeant, are you my friend?"

Simon shifted slightly and stared at the fire. "I have no friends."

Marcus chuckled and Denys roared with laughter. He pointed toward the chairs. "Please, gentlemen, sit. Can I get you anything?"

The Templar Knight shook his head. "No, thank you, sir. We must speak." He glanced over at the servant standing in the corner. "In private."

Denys waved a hand over his shoulder and the man

108

left the room, closing the door behind him. "I assume then that this isn't a friendly visit."

"I'm afraid not, sir. We have a situation. A friend of ours, Thomas Durant, is missing in most curious circumstances, circumstances that may involve Templars, though certainly none that are sanctioned."

Denys leaned back, a finger tapping his chin. "Yes, I remember this young man. And how long has he been missing?"

"Since two nights ago."

"And you're certain he's the victim of foul play?"

"Absolutely. We have a witness. Have you ever heard of opium?"

Denys tensed as much as his overly relaxed body could. He debated for a brief moment whether he should plead ignorance, but this was a man who he owed his life to, and if there were ever any way he could repay the debt he owed him, it would be by always being honest. "Yes, I have."

"Are you aware it's in Paris?"

"I was recently made aware of the fact about a week ago. How is the disappearance of Thomas connected to opium?"

"Thomas works for a woman named Mrs. Thibault. She has a debtor named Mr. Chapon, a baker in Thomas' neighborhood. He began missing payments for his loan two weeks ago, so Mrs. Thibault asked Thomas to follow him to find out where his money was going. Thomas did so, and was captured by the men who were running a local opium…lounge, shall we say?"

Denys gripped the arms of his chair, his knuckles turning white. "And this lounge, as you described it, was it perhaps underneath a clothing shop, one that would appear out of place in the slums of Paris?"

Marcus' eyebrows shot up and Simon's jaw dropped as he muttered a surprised curse. "How could you possibly know that?"

"Because I've been to this place just this week."

"What were you doing there?"

"Trying this opium you speak of. Some friends and I went to see what it was all about."

"So, you've used this?"

"Yes, I have. In fact, I was just using it when you arrived."

Marcus' eyes flared. "You have it here?"

"I do. I went to this lounge only the one time and found it quite unappealing, though the effects of the opium were quite the opposite. I made arrangements through a friend to have everything I would need brought here."

"I must insist, sir, that you stop using it immediately."

Denys shifted in his chair. "Why?"

"If you saw the baker, you wouldn't ask that question. It would appear that using this makes you become dependent upon it."

"You mean like an alcoholic?"

"Yes, though far worse. If you value your life, and your reputation, you will immediately stop using it."

Denys stared at his hands. "Is the shaking of one's hands a symptom of this affliction?"

"From what I've observed, yes."

"Then I fear I may have already become dependent upon it, for this morning my hands were shaking quite uncontrollably."

"How long have you been using it?"

"This morning was only the third time."

"Then perhaps it's not too late. Destroy anything you have. It may be difficult at first, but you'll get through it, I'm certain."

"Excuse me for a moment." He rose, the Templars rising with him in respect. He left the room and rushed back up the stairs and into his bedroom. He stared at the accouterments he had spent so much on, that had brought him such joy. He picked them up and flung them into the fire, the lamp and bowl shattering, the pipe slowly turning to flame. He took the pouch with the opium and tossed it in, then prayed that the choice he had just made was the correct one, and that it was a choice not made too late.

He returned to his guests and sat. "I fear many in the Court will have to heed the same advice. I must get word to them today."

Marcus frowned. "I would ask that you wait until we find Thomas."

"But these are my friends and colleagues. If what you say is true, any delay could be harmful."

"Then give us until this evening."

He sighed. "Very well. Most are due in court regardless. But you are here for a specific reason, not divine providence to save my life. How may I help you?"

Marcus beckoned Simon with a finger and the sergeant rose, presenting Denys with a cushion, the stuffing removed, that had previously gone unnoticed sitting beside him.

"What's this?"

"We found it in a corner of the lounge. It appeared to be a private setup. It has a coat of arms on one side we were hoping you could identify. It looks familiar to me, but I can't place it."

Denys flipped the cushion over and his eyes shot wide.

"Do you recognize it?"

"Of course I recognize it. This is the personal coat of arms of Prince Louis."

Marcus' eyebrows rose. "Prince Louis? The brother of the King?"

"Indeed. And if he's involved, this becomes a very delicate affair. What had you hoped to achieve in identifying this coat of arms?"

"We were hoping that because this person was likely nobility, the proprietors would contact him after they moved their operation, so that one of their best customers would be kept supplied. We were hoping to follow him to their new location, where we believe Thomas is being held."

"And your intention is merely to rescue Thomas?"

"No, it's our primary goal, of course, however, if Templars are involved, they must be stopped. No one in our order can be associated with such a sinful practice."

"I understand. But if you are caught following the Prince, it could bring trouble for your order. The King has never been your fan nor your order's."

"Yes. The fact that it is the Prince does pose an unforeseen risk. Do you have any suggestions?"

Denys smiled slightly. "As a matter of fact, I do."

Durant Residence
Paris, Kingdom of France

Jeremy stepped into the alleyway behind Thomas' house with Tanya. She bolted up the narrow road and he whistled. She returned immediately then stopped, dropping a deuce in the middle of the alley before rushing back to him, her tail wagging happily. He gave her a scratch behind the ears then smacked her rump, sending her back inside the humble home. He was about to follow her when he saw movement at the other end of the alleyway. He peered into the shadows and a young boy sprinted away. Jeremy cursed and stepped back inside, closing the door behind him. He made his way to the front of the house where everyone was gathered.

"We may have a problem."

"What?" asked David

"I just saw somebody in the alleyway. He ran away as soon as he realized I had seen him."

"What did he look like?"

"It was a young boy."

Chapon gasped. "That's what Sir Marcus said. He said they paid children to watch people."

David frowned. "It would make sense that they'd have somebody watching Thomas' house. They likely knew the moment you arrived here."

"Then we're not safe."

"No, we're not. There are only three of us to defend you, and if they come in numbers, we won't stand a

113

chance."

"Then what should we do?"

"I fear our chances are worse on the street than they are in here."

"We could try to get to the Fortress," suggested Jeremy. "It's not that far from here, and we have several horses."

Chapon shook his head vigorously. "No, I don't want to go to that place. I don't trust the Templars right now."

Jeremy wanted to defend his order, however held his tongue after David gave him a look. He instead offered another suggestion. "Do we believe that Sir Denys will offer them his protection?"

"I can't see that he wouldn't," replied David.

"Then perhaps we should go there now, under the assumption that his hospitality has already been granted."

"We could, however it's even farther than the Fortress. If they are indeed outside in numbers, we'll never make it."

"Then what would you suggest?" asked Chapon.

"I fear the only choice we have is to wait for Sir Marcus to return. We must be prepared to defend ourselves." David turned to Enzo. "Are you armed?"

"Merely with this knife, sir." He brandished the weapon.

"And you know how to use it?"

"Since I was six, sir."

"Then it's your job to protect these people inside. Jeremy and I will go to the roof with our bows. If anyone approaches, we'll take them down and hopefully make them think twice about taking us on."

"What if they have archers of their own?"

"Then we may not last long, and if they have torches, it will be a very short fight. Let's just pray that Sir Marcus arrives in time with help."

En Route to Durant Residence
Paris, Kingdom of France

Marcus rode with Simon on his left and Sir Denys de Montfort on his right, leading a column of the nobleman's personal guard. The streets were filled with the throngs of the capital, making the going slower than he would have liked. All they had to do was reach Thomas' house. Once they did, Isabelle and the Chapon family would be safe until their return to Denys' estate—no one would dare take on a dozen men on horseback led by a Templar Knight and his sergeant.

He glanced at Denys as the nobleman pulled slightly ahead. His face was dripping with sweat, and he appeared to be favoring his stomach as if battling the urge to vomit. Marcus was stunned he was in such bad shape after only three sessions of inhaling the opium. He had heard the stories when he was stationed in the Holy Land, but had paid them little attention. These were the problems of sinners, and sinners weren't his concern. Yet now he realized how this vile substance affected all those around it, including the innocent baker who had become dependent upon it, nearly destroying his family, nearly getting himself killed, and getting Thomas kidnapped or worse in the process. And now this nobleman, whom he knew to be a good and honorable man, was afflicted as well, along with an unknown number of his fellow members of the King's Court, the very people who managed the affairs of millions of people.

This substance destroyed the lives of those who

used it, and the lives of those connected to its victims. He had to stop it, and unfortunately, his best lead was Prince Louis, the brother of a king who despised the Templar Order simply because he owed an exorbitant sum to the wealthy organization. If the King were to catch wind the Templars were behind this, he would no doubt use that information to his advantage. And if something were to happen to his brother, he might make a move against the Order. This was quickly spiraling out of control. No longer was the life of young Thomas the only thing at stake. The very future of the Order he had dedicated his life to was as well.

Simon pointed ahead. "Look."

Marcus adjusted his gaze and his heart pounded at the sight of smoke in the direction they were heading. He urged his horse to move a little faster, yelling at the throngs on the roads to get out of the way.

Durant Residence
Paris, Kingdom of France

David spotted a man approaching the front door to Thomas' house. He had no weapons, but his furtive glances over both shoulders suggested he was nervous about being watched. David drew his bowstring tight, taking aim at the man's chest, waiting for something untoward to happen. He continued toward the door when someone shouted, "Above you!" The man looked up and spotted him, then reached under his long jacket, the hilt of a sword appearing. David loosed his arrow and his aim was true, the man dropping where he stood, another arrow already in place as David scanned the crowds for who had delivered the warning.

"I have two back here," announced Jeremy from behind him. He acknowledged the report but held his position. Two men were no problem for an archer. He heard the distinctive snap of Jeremy loosing one arrow, quickly followed by another. "Two down."

"Warn the others to be ready to run, then get back up here as quickly as possible."

Jeremy climbed down from the roof and through the second-floor window. He heard his friend's shouts and Enzo's acknowledgment, as well as cries of fear from the children.

"I'm back."

David continued to scan, wiping from his eyes the heavy sleet that was now falling. He was feeling slightly better now that Jeremy was watching his back, though couldn't relax knowing more were out there. "Where are you, you bastard?" He peered into the dark of an alley across the street. Something had caught his eye. A man emerged with a torch, the top aflame. He took several steps toward Thomas' house, his arm swinging back in preparation to throw what was now a weapon.

David loosed his arrow and the man dropped the torch, collapsing to the frozen ground. Another rushed from the shadows and grabbed it as David fit another arrow into position. He took aim as a carriage blocked his shot, then cursed as the torch sailed through the air. It hit the front of the building and he leaned over to see where it had ultimately fallen when someone on the street screamed and he returned his attention to the crowds. Two more people, barely men, whipped torches toward the home.

He drew his arrow, but hesitated. His target was merely a teenager and was already sprinting away. These were the children spoken of under the employ of those behind the opium infestation, and were merely desperate souls struggling to survive, their jobs likely already completed. A lick of flames rushed up the wall and he knew the battle was already lost.

He headed to the back of the house where Jeremy was. "We're done here." Jeremy cursed and they both climbed down from the roof and back into the house. David rushed down the stairs and found Isabelle and the others huddled together in the main living area, smoke filling the room. "We have to go. Now!"

"But they're out there!" she cried. "We'll die!"

"We'll die for sure if we stay in here."

Enzo hauled open the front door, flames flashing inside before settling. "It's not safe to go out the front." As if to punctuate his assessment, flames began licking the ceiling overhead.

David grabbed Isabelle by the hand. "Everyone out the back. Now." Chapon and his wife each grabbed a child and Enzo herded the entire group, his arms spread wide, as they all fled for their lives. David threw open the back door and stared down both ends of the alleyway. One end was clear, the other held the bodies of the two men that Jeremy had taken down earlier, the far end now blocked by four men. He urged everyone out then headed toward the empty end of the alleyway. Two men on horses appeared, swords drawn, blocking their only means of escape.

Tanya growled as Jeremy drew an arrow from his quiver and prepared for what appeared to be a hopeless battle.

Approaching the Durant Residence
Paris, Kingdom of France

Marcus now had no doubt the fire was from Thomas' neighborhood, and with what was going on, he was already convinced that it was the young man's house. If it were under attack in numbers, David, Jeremy, and Enzo stood little chance to defend the others. He was at a gallop now. The pounding of the hooves of over a dozen horses and the screams of those in their path provided a warning for those ahead, and the crowds were quickly parting. There was no time to waste anymore with polite beseechments to clear the way.

They rounded the final bend and found Thomas' childhood home aflame, the entire front of the building engulfed in an angry fire, smoke billowing into the late morning sky as a heavy sleet soaked the area. He scanned the crowds as he came to a halt, not spotting his friends or their charges.

A fire brigade had formed, the locals rushing with buckets filled with water from the local well, struggling to douse the flames before they spread to the all too close buildings next to the residence.

"Do you see them?" he asked Simon.

Simon shook his head. "No. Could they have escaped already?"

"Possibly, though if they did, from what I can tell, they would have gone out the back." He turned to Denys. "Stay here with six of your men. We're going to check the back."

"Very well." Denys directed his troops and Marcus

turned his horse, heading back down the street and around the corner. He turned into the alleyway that led to the rear of Thomas' home where he found several bodies, leaving little doubt his hunch of their escape route had been correct.

He peered through the dim light and saw the smoke billowing into the alleyway, and cursed as he saw the Chapon family huddled against the far wall. David and Jeremy held positions on opposite sides, and the massive bulk of Enzo lay on the ground, unmoving. The clash of swords overwhelmed the sounds of the fire and the battle raging out on the street as his squires fought, having abandoned their bows and turned to swords. Tanya was at the far end, barking and snarling at two men on horseback, their skittish horses rearing up on their hindlegs in panic.

Marcus hadn't wasted a moment during his assessment of the situation, instead charging forward, his sword extended in front of him, Simon at his side. Their foes finally noticed and turned to face the new threat, but it was too late for them. Marcus swung his sword, cleaving his target at the shoulder, the man's arm falling off as he screamed in agony. Simon continued past as Marcus brought his sword back for another swing. The blade swept through the air over the heads of the cowering Chapon family, removing the head of another hostile as Jeremy ducked just in time. The sight of the half-dozen mounted personal guard following the two Templars was enough to put the fear of God into those that remained, and they quickly beat a hasty retreat as Marcus and Simon chased them down, removing them from God's green earth.

Marcus stopped at the far end of the alley, making

certain there wouldn't be a second wave, then he and Simon returned to where David and Jeremy were now tending to Enzo, Tanya happily following as if nothing had happened. "Is he all right?"

"He took a blow to the head that knocked him out cold, but he's fine."

Simon grunted. "I never would have thought a man such as this could be knocked out."

"Nor I," agreed Marcus.

Jeremy pointed at one of the now riderless horses. "Take a look at his opponent."

Marcus chuckled. "Only a horse could best a man such as this." He glanced over his shoulder at the smoke now filling the alleyway. "All right, everybody, let's move to the street!"

David and Jeremy grabbed Enzo and hauled him to his feet, each carrying him by an arm over their shoulders, the effort clear from the grimaces on their faces. Marcus and Simon covered the retreat as the personal guard led the way to safety. They merged with Denys' group on the main street and the spare horses brought along for the purpose. David and Jeremy helped Isabelle and the Chapon family onto the animals, the panic in everyone's eyes clear, tears flowing down poor Isabelle's face as she stared at what was to have been her future home. Marcus wanted to comfort the girl, yet now wasn't the time. He instead positioned himself on one side of her, Simon on the opposite, determined to protect her from any further harm, emotional or physical, as they left the area surrounded by Denys' personal guard.

As they left the danger behind them, Marcus realized that the foe they faced was far more vicious and far more violent than he had anticipated. And if they were members of his order, he would show them no quarter, and would gut them from belly to chin without hesitation for having put those he loved at risk.

Thibault Residence
Paris, Kingdom of France

Thibault sat behind her ornate desk, feeling more alone and more insecure than she had for as long as she could remember. Enzo hadn't shown up this morning, and it had her concerned. It was unlike him. The only reason he wouldn't be here was if something had gone wrong. If Templars were indeed involved, they could be a ruthless bunch when threatened. She prayed to a god she feared more than most for her friend's safety, for he was all she had in this world beyond Thomas. Her chest ached at the thought, for at this moment, the only two people she had any feelings for could be dead.

And then what would she do?

She would be alone and unprotected. There were other beasts of men like Enzo in the slums that would be happy to work for her, though the bond she shared with Enzo, the trust that was there, the loyalty, would be something hard-earned, and it would take years to establish. Someone like Thomas was rare in these parts, and though she had only known him for mere months, she sensed that she would miss him more than the lumbering beast she considered her only friend.

She sighed, staring through the door and down the hallway to where the young man would normally be sitting, toiling away at the books.

I'm so alone.

A wave of self-pity swept over her, yet it was her fault. She had chosen this way of life. She shook her head, for that wasn't entirely true. She had chosen this

125

way of life with her husband. They were supposed to be in this together, they were supposed to be each other's best friends. But he had died and left her alone.

Completely alone.

Yes, she could walk into any tavern, splash a little money around for drinks, and be feted as the great dame of the neighborhood. But it was all fake. None of it was real. These people would treat her like gold as long as they were getting something from her for free. And with Enzo standing in the corner, his arms folded across his massive chest, they wouldn't dare not pretend to at least enjoy her company. It was good for the moment it lasted, though when they thought no one was looking, someone always rolled their eyes or made some snide remark that she would catch. And despite being perceived as a cold-hearted bitch, it hurt nonetheless. Sometimes she would go home and lie in her empty bed, weeping for God to take her so she could be reunited with her long lost husband.

And every morning she would awaken, alive and well, a renewed punishment from a god who would see her suffer rather than enjoy the peace death might bring her.

Someone rapped heavily on the door down the stairs, and she flinched, her heart hammering as she remembered her protector wasn't there. She rose and walked through the house, peering out the front window down at the street below, and spotted a young man in a Templar squire's brown tunic. Her heart leaped into her throat for a moment before she recognized who it was. She opened the window and leaned out.

"What do you want?"

The man looked up. "Mrs. Thibault, it's Jeremy, squire to Sir Marcus de Rancourt. He wishes that you accompany me immediately. Enzo has been hurt."

Her eyes flooded with tears and her chest tightened as her stomach became a fit of knots. She said nothing, instead closing the window as she rushed back to her chambers and readied herself. Moments later, she was down the stairs and out the door to find Jeremy already on his horse, a second at his side. He handed her the reins and she mounted the beast. He took off without saying a word and she followed, catching up to him.

"Is he all right?"

"He'll survive, but with what just happened, Sir Marcus felt it best you were brought to a safe location until things are resolved."

A wave of weakness swept through her body and she leaned over in her saddle. A strong hand, gripping her arm, brought her back to her senses.

"Are you all right?"

She patted the hand that had saved her from tumbling from her saddle. "Yes, I'll be fine. Your words were just a shock." She drew a deep breath, steadying her nerves. "So, it *is* Templars we're dealing with?"

He shook his head. "We don't know. All we do know is that they came in numbers and attempted to kill Mr. Chapon and his family along with a friend of mine, Isabelle."

"Thomas' young love. Is she unharmed?"

"Yes. We managed to save them all, but in the process of defending them, Enzo was charged by a horse and knocked out. He's fine now and being tended to, but he asked for Sir Marcus to protect you, so it was decided you should be brought to his location."

127

He had them at a gallop, shouting at the unaware ahead of them to get out of the way, several narrowly missed.

"Is this speed really necessary?" she asked, unaccustomed to riding a horse in such a manner.

He jerked a thumb over his shoulder. "You tell me."

She glanced behind them and gasped. Two men on horseback were charging after them, quickly closing the gap. "We'll never outrun them."

"We don't have to. Just keep up with me."

He continued their breakneck charge and she mimicked him, leaning forward in the saddle, urging the creature she rode to hurry. They came around a bend and Jeremy pulled up on his reins. She looked ahead to see what might have him doing such a foolish thing, but could see no reason until another Templar squire she recognized stepped into the road, his bow raised. Jeremy leaped from his saddle, swinging his own bow from his back and fitting an arrow.

"Two on horseback," he informed David.

The riders pursuing them rounded the bend and two arrows were loosed immediately, both men collapsing in their saddles then falling from their horses. Someone screamed and the crowds scurried away in a panic.

"Are you sure that's all of them?" asked David as he readied another arrow.

"All that I saw."

"Then let's get out of here before more come looking for them."

Jeremy mounted his horse and David disappeared into an alleyway, emerging a moment later on his own. "Let's go, Mrs. Thibault, before more arrive."

She followed the two squires, the pace a little more reasonable this time, and gave Jeremy a look. "You could have at least told me what was going on."

He grinned. "It wouldn't have been nearly as dramatic if I had."

De Montfort Estate
Paris, Kingdom of France

Marcus watched as Isabelle and one of Denys' chambermaids tended to the massive Enzo. He was awake now and well aware of his surroundings, and Marcus had a feeling the big man was prolonging his suffering to enjoy the ministrations of the two young, beautiful women. Simon cleared his throat behind him and Marcus glanced over his shoulder.

"We're ready."

"All right. I'll be down in a moment."

Isabelle turned toward him. "Go ahead. Don't worry about us. We're safe here. Go and find my Thomas."

He bowed. "I will do my best." He closed the door and followed Simon down the hallway and then the stairs. Mrs. Thibault stood there with David and Jeremy. "Any problems?"

"Not really," replied David.

Thibault gave him a look. "Not really? Two men chased us on horseback and nearly killed us."

David shrugged. "Like I said, not really. We anticipated the move and set a trap for them. There was little danger to Mrs. Thibault."

She rolled her eyes. "If that's what you consider little danger, I fear the day I experience true danger with you. Now, where is my Enzo?"

Marcus indicated the stairs behind him. "Up the stairs and to the left, last door on the right."

She was off in a flash, calling Enzo's name as she rushed toward her enforcer. Marcus was genuinely touched by the concern in her voice.

Perhaps she's not so bad after all.

Denys entered the room. "I must go to the Palace now."

"Will you have an opportunity to speak to Prince Louis?"

"No, it would be quite unusual if I were to do so. However, there should be no need. If your intention is to follow him, all we need to know is that he is at the Palace. Once I've determined that, I'll have word sent. If he is indeed in court, when it is finished, he will leave in his personal carriage with his coat of arms on its side, through the rear entrance. If you position yourselves there, you should have no problem following him. But try not to be seen in those outfits, because he, like his brother, has no love of the Templars, and will be very suspicious if members of your order are spotted following him."

"Understood. We will await your word."

De Montfort Estate
Paris, Kingdom of France

"Enzo! Where is my Enzo?"

"In here, ma'am!"

Thibault sighed in relief at her enforcer's voice. She threw open the door to find the man lying in a bed designed for someone far smaller, his feet hanging off the end, his shoulders extending from edge to edge. He struggled to get up to show her the respect he always did, but she waved him off. "Stay down, stay down." He slumped back in the bed and a chambermaid, as well as a young woman she presumed was Thomas' Isabelle, returned to stroking his hair and wiping down his face. Thibault found a tiny sliver of the bed not occupied by his massive frame, and perched on it, frowning at the bandaged head. "I hear you had a run-in with a horse."

"Quite literally, ma'am."

"I'm surprised you came out on the losing end of that."

He chuckled. "As am I, ma'am."

"How do you feel?"

"I'm fine. I can return to duty now if you want."

She shook her head and patted his arm. "We'll be staying here until this is over. Sir Denys has a personal guard that will protect everyone, including me. You relax. Get your rest."

"Thank you, ma'am. Any news of Thomas?"

"None, beyond the fact he's still missing. I do believe Sir Marcus has a plan to find him."

"Tell him I'm ready to help should he need it. We have to save that boy."

"I will." She sighed. "If something happens to him, I'll never forgive myself."

Enzo's eyes flared briefly at her emotional display. "I'm sure he's fine, ma'am."

"I pray you're right. Will you be all right here in the company of these two lovely ladies?"

He flashed a grin. "Absolutely."

Isabelle giggled and slapped him gently on the shoulder. "You're terrible, Enzo."

Thibault smiled at how happy her only friend appeared to be. This was probably the first time in his life that any young, attractive women had paid him any mind voluntarily. She let him have his moment. "I'll be downstairs if you need me. I must speak with Sir Marcus and see what this plan is he's hatched."

"Very well, ma'am."

She left the room and returned to where the others were gathered. Denys nodded to her then left the room, dressed for outdoors. "I hope it was nothing I said."

Marcus smiled slightly and indicated a chair in which to sit. She sat, then Marcus and Simon did as well, the two squires that had saved her life standing to the side. "Sir Denys is off to the Palace now. We hope to have word from him shortly on the next stage of our plan."

"And what exactly is this plan?"

"First, it was to secure Mr. Chapon and his family as well as yourself."

"And you barely succeeded, from what your squires told me."

"True."

"And the second part of your plan?"

"Now we must endeavor to discover where Thomas is being held."

"And it is your belief that he's alive?"

"There are no guarantees, however I do believe he is, though he may not be for long. I fear if we don't find him before the day is out, we may never find him."

"Do you have any idea where they might be?"

"No. They knew we were coming last night, so they abandoned their location below the clothing shop in your neighborhood before we could get there."

Thibault's eyes narrowed. "The clothing shop? Huh. I always wondered about that place, about how it could possibly stay in business. I've been inside on several occasions."

Marcus' eyebrows rose slightly. "You've been inside?"

"Of course. I'm one of the few in the area that can afford what they sell. What I found surprising was how many members of the nobility frequented there."

"I'm surprised any dare venture into the neighborhood."

"You'd be surprised how many of the rich get a thrill from seeing how much better their lives are than the majority of those they rule. They arrive in their horse-drawn carriages, helped out by their servants, then doted upon inside where they're shown fashions that are available nowhere else in the city, even the lowliest of scarves out of the reach of the denizens they then flaunt their newly acquired extravagances in front of. It is quite the sight, quite the delight."

"A delight of which you are guilty of as well, are you not?"

She smiled. "Absolutely, but I don't pretend to be something I am not. I am not nobility, I don't rule the masses. I merely provide a service, and in order to show how successful I am at that service, so that I might attract other customers, I must play the part of the successful widow."

"And you don't fear the resentment your display of wealth might bring?"

"That's what I have Enzo for."

"But do you not think you would sleep better at night if so many didn't hate you?"

Her chest tightened as the lie was spoken. "I've never concerned myself with such things."

Marcus stared into her eyes for a moment. "I don't believe you. I heard you running up those stairs. You have a heart, Mrs. Thibault. It may be buried deeply, but it is a heart nonetheless."

She shifted in her seat, suddenly uncomfortable, and decided changing the subject would be best. "Back to your plan to find Thomas. How do you propose to do so?"

Marcus continued. "Very well. While we were in the basement of the clothing shop, we searched the place and discovered a cushion with a coat of arms embroidered on it."

Simon held it up then tossed it back on the chair beside him.

Her eyes flared with fear. "That's Prince Louis' personal coat of arms."

"You recognize it?"

"Of course I do. Anyone who lives in Paris knows that crest, and knows that if you see it to keep your distance, and if at all possible, leave its presence."

"The Prince has a reputation?"

"He does indeed. As the brother of the King, laws don't apply to him. At least that's what he believes. He has been known to run down people with his horse or with his carriage. If he sees a woman he fancies, he's been known to have his people grab her off the street. He is a vile sort. That one partakes far too much in drink and other forms of debauchery."

"Then you wouldn't be surprised that he too is a user of this opium?"

"Not in the slightest. If there is something sinful to partake in, then he would certainly be involved."

"From what we observed, we believe he is not only a frequent customer of those involved, but perhaps one of their best. It's our belief that they would make certain he was well aware of their new location after they moved. We're hoping he will go to the new location after court today. We intend to follow him and hopefully rescue Thomas should he be held there."

"And what of the Templar involvement? What are you going to do about that?"

Marcus frowned. "I'm not as certain of that."

"Yet should it be true?"

"I won't rest until I've put a stop to it."

"And should it be sanctioned by your order?"

"I find that impossible to believe, however again, should it be true, I will stop at nothing to put an end to it."

"Even if it should cost your order its future?"

He stared at her. "Yes, even if it should cost my order its future."

THE BLACK SCOURGE

Palais de la Cité
Paris, Kingdom of France

Denys clasped his hands behind his back in an attempt to steady the shaking. Sweat beaded on his forehead and his stomach churned, his entire body racked with pain. If this lasted much longer, he wasn't certain how he would cope. He had barely used the opium three times, and was already so afflicted, that he craved it intensely. He had been told the first time he tried it that it affected everyone differently, though no mention had been made of the torture that could result. If he had known, if he had any inkling that suffering such as this could be the result, he never would have tried it.

Alcohol was a known quantity. If he abused it, he would pay the price the next day, and the day after, he would be fine. He had seen those who partook far too frequently, and they too appeared to suffer as he did now. He would never again look upon them with the disdain he once did. They weren't weak-willed as he had once thought, they were merely dependent upon something that had consumed their souls, as his was now.

He spotted Sir Benuche, the man who had introduced him to this hellish substance. He forced a smile and walked over to him and the small cluster of others, some of whom he knew for certain were users of opium.

Benuche smiled then frowned, concern on his face. "Sir Denys, are you not well?"

"I'm feeling a little under the weather today." Denys

noted a couple of the others seemed similarly afflicted, including Benuche.

"Perhaps you should partake in some of the indulgence we enjoyed together last week. I find I always feel better after I do."

Denys decided a lie was best after what he had been told earlier. "I would have, however I've unfortunately run out."

Benuche's eyebrows shot up. "Already? Did you not have a full supply brought to you just a couple of days ago?"

Denys forced a sheepish smile. "I'm afraid I shared some of it with friends. It's always more pleasurable to experience these things among the company of others."

Benuche chuckled. "Yes, indeed it is."

Denys took a risk. "On that note, I went to our friends to acquire more product last night, however I found no one there. Do you know where I might find them?"

A bell was rung, indicating the start of court. Benuche patted him on the arm. "See me afterward. I'll make sure you're taken care of."

Denys smiled. "Thank you." He followed the others into the Court to await the arrival of the King. He scanned the faces near the front of the massive room. The more senior the member of the Court one was, the closer one was allowed to get to the King, and he smiled at the sight of Prince Louis standing with his entourage of professional ass kissers. Now all he had to do was find an opportunity to get a message to Marcus to confirm that their plan could proceed.

De Montfort Estate
Paris, Kingdom of France

Marcus paced in front of the fire with growing impatience. He was a man of action, and sitting here waiting for word was unbearable. And once that word arrived, even should it be in their favor, it would merely signal that hours from then, they could perhaps take action. He figured they had at least six hours of the day before their plan could proceed.

He spun on his heel and faced Simon, his sergeant picking his nails with the tip of his dagger. "Are you interested in going for a ride?"

Simon leaped to his feet. "Does Jerusalem smell like ass in the summer?"

Marcus laughed. "It does indeed."

"Just what did you have in mind?"

"With everyone safe here, I'd like to survey the damage to Thomas' home, and then pay another visit to that clothing shop. Perhaps there is something we've missed that might be revealed in the light of day."

David stepped forward. "May we join you?"

"No, I need you to stay here in case the message arrives. Should it, you know where we'll be. Have Jeremy come find us."

David bowed. "Yes, sir. May I suggest you take Tanya with you? She needs to get outside, and she can prove to be a good deterrent should the need arise."

Tanya, lying on the hearth in front of the fire, perked up at the mention of her name. "No, not this time. Discretion may be required. Prepare our horses. We'll be leaving at once."

"Yes, sir." David and Jeremy left the room as Marcus and Simon climbed the stairs, each heading for their respective rooms. A servant at the end of the hall stepped forward.

"Do you require anything, sir?"

"Yes. I'll need you to help me into my armor."

"Absolutely, sir." The man followed Marcus into his room and expertly assisted him as capably as any squire.

"Did you serve in the Crusades?" asked Marcus.

"I did indeed, sir. For five years. My master was unfortunately killed, and I returned home with the others. Sir Denys was kind enough to offer me a position."

"You serve him well."

"Thank you, sir."

Marcus inspected his armor, raising his hands above his head and twisting from side to side, making certain he had a full range of motion. He nodded to the man. "Good work."

"Thank you, sir."

Marcus left his room and returned to the sitting area, finding it empty. He grabbed the cushion cover with Prince Louis' coat of arms, then headed for the stables where David and Jeremy had the horses prepared. Simon joined them a few moments later, struggling with one of his arms.

"Jeremy, can you look at this? The fool who dressed me has no experience."

Jeremy attended to his sergeant, resolving the problem within moments. Simon made a full rotation

140

with his arm and grunted his approval. "Much better."

Jeremy smiled. "You're welcome."

Simon gave him a look. "The expectation of manners can get you a backhanded thank you." He held up his fist to emphasize his point. Jeremy scurried away in mock fear, making the final adjustments to the saddle of the horse he had been tending.

"You're all set, sir," said David. "I'll have Jeremy get word to you the moment we hear anything."

Marcus handed Simon the cushion cover. "Put this in your saddlebags. We may need it."

Simon eyed it then packed it. "I'm not going to ask why."

They both mounted their horses, and less than half an hour later were in the now familiar neighborhood that Thomas and Isabelle were hoping to call home for half the year, though with the fire he had seen, he feared those plans might at best be delayed, and at worst, completely scuttled.

As they rounded the final bend toward Thomas' home, his eyes shot wide in surprise. The facade of the home was indeed destroyed, though the rest of the structure appeared in reasonable condition. He dismounted, holding the reins of his horse as he examined the area. A man stepped out from inside.

"What business do you have here?" His eyes widened slightly as he caught sight of Marcus' white surcoat with red cross emblazoned on it. "Oh, sorry, sir. You must be the friends of Thomas I've heard talk of."

Marcus bowed slightly. "We are indeed friends of Thomas."

"My name is Richart." He extended a hand and

141

Marcus accepted it. "Have you seen him? We've been trying to find him but have been unsuccessful. No one has seen him in two days. My family and I have been watching the house since the fire to make certain no one loots the place, however there's only so much we can do."

"We appreciate your efforts, as I'm sure Thomas does as well." Marcus stared at the house. "How bad is the damage inside?"

"The structure is sound, though everything has been damaged by smoke. It will need a good airing out and a good scrubbing down, and of course the front will need to be rebuilt. If I had some funds, I could purchase some wood to at least board up the place until Thomas returns. I'm a carpenter by trade."

Marcus smiled slightly. "As I'm sure you're aware, Templars are forbidden from carrying more than four deniers on their person, otherwise I would happily hand over whatever funds you would require. If my word is sufficient, then please make your purchases on credit, and I will have the money you require before the end of tomorrow."

Richart regarded him for a moment. "I suppose if I can't trust the word of a Templar monk, then I can't trust the word of anybody."

"You honor me, sir."

Richart turned to another, much younger. "Do you know what we need?"

"Yes, Father."

"See Mr. Venyse. Tell him I sent you, and what you heard here. Have everything delivered here as quickly as possible. I want this place secure before night falls."

"Yes, Father." The young man rushed off and

Marcus turned to Richart.

"I will make certain that you receive your money by tomorrow, and once we find Thomas, make certain he knows it was you who helped protect his family home."

"Thank you, sir." Richart stared at his feet for a moment. "If you would like, I can organize some of the neighbors, and we can begin to rebuild the home should Thomas wish to return."

"I know it's his desire to stay here with the woman he would marry, so if you and your neighbors are willing, you have my blessing, and promise of funds to take care of the repairs."

Richart smiled. "It would be an honor. I knew Thomas' parents. They were good people, especially his mother, and I know she weeps from Heaven at the sight before us today."

Marcus mounted his horse. "I wish you a good day, sir."

The man bowed and Marcus guided his horse toward the clothing shop as the man ran after his son.

Simon rode up beside him. "And just where are we getting these funds to rebuild Thomas' house?"

"I believe that Mrs. Thibault will be in a very giving mood."

Simon chuckled. "Because she's always been known to be a generous soul."

Palais de la Cité
Paris, Kingdom of France

The King rose and all in the Court bowed. He departed through his own private entrance behind the throne as the proceedings paused for the midday meal. Rather than take his customary seat at the long tables brought out by the servants, Denys disappeared into the halls and flagged down a messenger. He was handed a pen and paper and he quickly jotted down a cryptic message to Marcus in the event it was intercepted, a simple message of a single word.

Yes.

He folded the page and the messenger poured candle wax where the folds met, and Denys pressed his ring into the rapidly cooling substance. "Have this delivered to my estate immediately."

"Yes, sir." The messenger rushed off and Denys collapsed against the wall, his entire body shaking.

"Sir Denys, are you all right?"

He flinched at Benuche's voice. "I fear I am not," he confessed, his mind not thinking clearly. This was a man who had connections to those who had attempted to murder an innocent family to keep their secret, and were peddling this vile substance that had him so ill, and would make others as equally ill.

He couldn't trust him.

"Should you require it, I have some opium in my carriage. I can have my man bring it inside and set it up in one of the private chambers. We can both enjoy a few peaceful moments before court returns, and I'm confident you'll be your normal self in short order."

The proposition sounded as sweet as honey, and he could imagine nothing more appealing. He was about to agree when he looked down at his trembling hands. He shook his head. "No, I'll be fine in a moment." He took a long breath, struggling to steady himself, remembering his purpose. "You said you had information on where I could find our friends again?"

Benuche patted him on the arm. "I do, but not here. I'll tell you when court closes, and you can arrange a new delivery."

Denys nodded. "I look forward to it."

Benuche walked away, leaving Denys leaning against the wall, his entire body racked by tremors, far worse than the most severe fever he had ever battled, and he wondered how he would ever make it through the day.

Outside the Clothing Shop
Paris, Kingdom of France

Marcus came to a halt in front of the shop, surprised to see a carriage waiting outside, a coat of arms on the door indicating nobility. Laughter could be heard inside, and Simon stared at him incredulously. "They're open!"

Marcus pursed his lips. "It would appear so."

"They're either bold or fools."

"One can be both."

"Should we wait?"

Marcus shook his head. "No, let's see how the proprietor reacts to the sight of us." He pointed at Simon's saddlebag. "Bring the cushion." Simon retrieved the cover then followed him up the steps. Marcus opened the door and stepped inside. The interior was light and cheerful, the walls painted white and covered in bright fabrics. All the windows were open, allowing the sunlight inside, despite the chill in the air. A large fire roared in the corner, the heat taking enough of the edge off for a young woman being doted upon to be comfortable enough to reveal far too much skin for a modest woman to be respected.

The gentleman accompanying her, easily thirty years her senior, turned to see who had entered and his eyes shot wide at the sight of their Templar tunics. He quickly turned his head as if afraid to be recognized, though he needn't have, as Marcus had no clue who the man was.

The woman playfully performed a seductive dance with a pink veil in front of her face, removing any doubt as to whether she was the man's daughter or mistress. And as Marcus scanned the interior of the shop, he realized exactly what this place was. Everything inside was made of sheer fabrics, likely from the Far East, the outfits certainly not lady-like. This place was where men brought their illicit lovers to spice up their romantic lives, and the connection with the operation beneath their feet became clear. Men who would cheat on their wives, men who would give in to the temptations of the flesh and sin before God, were likely the same type who might give in to the temptations of the scourge peddled beneath the floorboards upon which they now stood.

"It's time to go, my dear."

The young woman pouted then held up the veil. "Can we get this?"

"Of course, of course." Several coins were impatiently pressed into the proprietor's hand and the girl squealed with delight as they left with several bundles. The door slammed shut and the shopkeeper smiled at them as he assessed his new guests with an exaggerated stare.

"Are you lost, gentlemen?"

Marcus smiled slightly. "Not at all."

The man reached out and rubbed the rough fabric of Marcus' tunic between his fingers. "I'm not sure I carry anything in your style."

"We're not here to shop."

The man let go of the tunic. "Oh? Then why are you here?"

"I think you know," grumbled Simon.

The man regarded him. "I assure you, I have no

147

clue."

"We're here regarding your operation in the basement."

The man's eyes shot wide. "What operation?"

Simon took a step closer. "Are you going to play the fool?"

The man shrugged. "I am no fool, Sergeant, therefore I cannot play one. However, I can plead ignorance. I have no idea what the gentleman who rents my basement is up to. I assure you, however, that it is nothing nefarious, nothing criminal."

Marcus was slightly taken aback at the revelation the basement was rented. Could this man indeed be innocent? It would make sense. Reopening after abandoning an opium operation only the night before was foolhardy, to say the least, unless one had no involvement whatsoever. "You're telling me you're renting the basement?"

"I am."

"To whom?"

"I fail to see what business it is of yours to whom I rent my basement to."

"Are you aware of what they're doing down there?"

"As I already said, I'm not, though I've been assured it's nothing untoward."

"They've created an opium lounge."

"Opium? I'm not quite certain what that is."

"You've never heard of it?"

"I've heard the word. Isn't it some sort of Eastern medicine? I honestly cannot say I know much more beyond that."

"It's something you inhale that is quite

148

intoxicating."

The man's eyes widened slightly, his face brightening. "Like alcohol?"

"Similar, yes."

"It sounds delightful. Perhaps I shall pay him a visit tonight."

"I think you'll find that your renter will not be returning. He abandoned your basement last night."

The man's eyes narrowed. "Why would he do such a thing?"

"Because he kidnapped a friend of ours and attempted to kill one of his customers and his family."

The man's hand darted to his chest. "Oh my! Are they all right?"

"Yes, they are, however our friend is still missing."

Simon took another menacing step forward. "And if you know anything, you'll tell us now."

The man paled. "I swear to you, I know nothing."

"What is your renter's name?"

"Charles."

"His full name."

"I don't know, to be honest. He offered me a large sum of money to rent the basement on a weekly basis. It was too much to say no to. My shop wasn't doing very well at the time."

Marcus looked about. "Why would you choose such a location?"

"I had little money to open where those who could afford my wares might easily find me. My brother, whose purse was bigger than his brain, sold everything and traveled to the Holy Land to purchase much of what you see before you today. He returned with many fine silks and cloths, however, not a denier to his name. He died within weeks of arriving, leaving me all of this, our entire family's fortune. I managed to sell several of the silks, enough to scrape together the money to open this shop, then through a friend who arranged encounters between wealthy men and women of, shall we say, questionable virtue, put the word out of what I sold here. Soon, men of means began frequenting the establishment with their mistresses, and I thankfully have been able to slowly dig my family out of the hole my moronic elder brother created."

"And the basement?"

"When I rented this shop, it included the basement, though I wasn't using it. A man approached me shortly after my business started to become a success, and offered me more money than the rent on the entire building. I would have been a fool not to take it."

"And how would you describe this man?"

The proprietor shrugged. "About your height and build, perhaps your age. Average looking. Nothing distinctive, I'm afraid."

"When were you expecting to see him again?"

"His rent is due tonight, though if he has abandoned the location, as you say, then I suspect he will not show up."

"About what time would he normally be here?"

"Just after the close of business. At dusk."

"Very well. We'll return tomorrow to see what news you have."

"If you prefer, I can send you a message. Where are you staying? At the Templar Fortress?"

"That won't be necessary. We shall return tomorrow. Make no mention that we were here. It may put your life at risk."

The man paled again. "I-I understand."

Marcus turned to leave when he stopped and pointed at the cushion cover gripped in Simon's hand. "Do you recognize this coat of arms?"

Simon showed the man the cushion and he shook his head. "No, should I?"

"No, though if you recognized it, you'd realize how much danger you may be in. Like I said, tell no one we were here."

"You-you have my word."

Marcus bid the man adieu then left the shop, stepping down onto the muddy street, the midday sun and sleet earlier in the day slowly thawing the dirt.

"Do you believe him?"

Marcus chewed his cheek. "The man's story is plausible, though it's equally plausible he's lying, or at least knows more than he's admitting to."

"Do you believe there's actually a renter?"

"I'm not convinced either way." He mounted his horse. "Let's return to Thomas' house and help his neighbors with the repairs, then come back here to watch for this renter should he return."

"And shouldn't he?"

"Then either the man is telling the truth, or he himself is the renter of his own basement."

De Montfort Estate
Paris, Kingdom of France

Isabelle sat perched on the edge of a chair, wringing her hands, her mind preoccupied with the fate of the man she loved. David and Jeremy sat nearby, restocking their quivers with fresh arrows supplied by Denys' marshal. "Shouldn't we have heard something by now?"

David looked up. "To be honest, miss, I don't know. I have no knowledge of how the King's Court functions, though I wouldn't worry yet. It's barely midday, and I'm certain that if the Prince is in court today, he won't be leaving anytime soon. In fact, this may be the first opportunity for Sir Denys to send word, as I would suspect they break for the same midday meal we just enjoyed."

There was a knock at one of the doors to the room then a servant walked in balancing a tray. "I have a message from Sir Denys, addressed to Sir Marcus de Rancourt."

"I'll take that."

The man bowed slightly as David removed the folded page from the tray, then retreated from the room. David broke the seal and unfolded the paper. His eyes widened slightly.

"What does it say?" asked Jeremy.

"Yes."

"What?"

"That's all it says. 'Yes.'"

"What does that mean?"

"I take it to mean that Prince Louis is indeed in court." He folded the page back up and handed it to Jeremy. "Take this to Sir Marcus at once."

"Where should I look?"

"Take the same route to Thomas' house that we took coming here. If you don't find them there, then the only other place they should be is this clothing shop they spoke of. Ask Mr. Chapon for directions before you leave."

"And should I not find them in either location?"

"Then return here. If they don't hear from us, then this is their most likely destination as they know it's essential they be here in time to follow Prince Louis after he leaves the Palace."

Jeremy left the room to find Chapon, and Isabelle turned to David.

"I really wish Sir Marcus hadn't left like he did."

David shrugged. "He had his reasons, and it will be hours before he needs to return, regardless."

Thibault descended the stairs and Isabelle rose. "How's Enzo doing?"

"Very well. I think the gentle monster is enjoying the attention he's receiving a little too much."

Isabelle smiled. "Once you get past his…umm…"

"Face?"

She flushed. "Yes, face. He's actually a sweet man when he's not growling or yelling."

Thibault sat in one of the chairs. "This is true, however make sure you tell no one of this fact, otherwise he'll lose his effectiveness." She leaned to one side in her chair. "So, I understand you and

Thomas have reached an agreement as to how you would like to live your lives."

"Yes, we have, or rather we had. With the fire at his house, I fear we no longer have anywhere to stay in Paris."

Thibault frowned, staring at her as the tears flowed. "Fret not, little one. Should our Thomas be found alive, I will make certain that your future home is rebuilt."

Hope surged through Isabelle, a smile spreading. "You would do this for us?"

"I would. Thomas is important to me, and if you are to be his wife, then you are as well."

Her heart fluttered at the word.

Wife.

Oh, how she wanted to be Thomas' wife. She was desperate to get married, to have children, to start the family she had always dreamed of having, and though her plans were entirely different than they had been only six months before, she couldn't imagine being happier. Six months ago, her fantasy had her married to Marcus and bearing his children, while living on the farm she had grown up on. Now, she hoped to marry Thomas and split her time between the farm and the city she had always feared.

She sighed.

"What is it, little one."

"He hasn't formally asked me yet."

"He hasn't asked you what?"

"To marry him."

"Do you honestly expect a shy one such as that to ask you?"

Isabelle smiled sheepishly. "No, I suppose not.

154

What would you suggest?"

Thibault's eyes glistened as she stared into the distance. "When I grew impatient of my husband not asking me the same question, I merely sat him down and asked him what his intentions were. And when he faltered in answering, I asked, 'Do you intend to marry me?' and he said, 'Yes,' and I said, 'Good, then it's settled' The problem was solved, and we were married shortly thereafter. I suggest you do something similar, otherwise your hair will be turning gray before Thomas finds the courage to ask you on his own volition."

She smiled at the prospect. Her dream for over a decade had been Marcus taking a knee in front of her, then spouting something poetic and romantic before posing the question every young girl dreams of being asked. She would gush her acceptance, then he would rise, lifting her into the air and kissing her passionately. She swooned at the fantasy.

Then replaced Marcus with Thomas.

She could imagine him taking the knee, then he'd stumble upon any romantic words, and could never lift her into the air. The unromantic image had her tears flowing and her face beaming, removing any doubt her infatuation with Marcus was over and her love for Thomas and all of his flaws, was true and certain and unwavering.

She just prayed that the love she had been waiting so long to arrive, was still alive.

Durant Residence
Paris, Kingdom of France

Rebuilding the barn burned by suspicious villagers, then constructing from the ground up the barracks Marcus and his men now lived in, had prepared them well, allowing him and Simon to pitch in with the dozen or more neighbors repairing Thomas' house. The damage to the front was severe, though inside, the initial assessment by the carpenter Richart they had spoken to earlier appeared accurate. Everything was covered in smoke and such, but the damage from the flames was minimal.

A group of women and young girls were already inside scrubbing away, as the men worked on the exterior, the sleet the Good Lord having sent this morning saving Thomas' home from certain destruction, as well as perhaps half the neighborhood. The supplies had arrived swiftly, Richart's son efficient, the bill pressed into Marcus' hands the moment they dismounted. The amount was substantial, and he prayed Thibault would come through, though if she didn't, Denys might, but it was something he would hate to ask of the man.

Rather than board up the house temporarily, with the number of volunteers willingly working, they were quickly rebuilding the front, and he was confident they would be finished before the sun set. As he directed the rebuild along with Richart, he delighted in listening to the tales told of Thomas' parents and his childhood. He was quite certain that Thomas had no idea how well-loved they had been all these years, though he suspected when they did finally find him and he returned home to see what his neighbors had done for him, any doubt he had would be removed.

"Sir Marcus!"

Marcus turned to see Jeremy galloping toward him, and his heart picked up a few beats as he climbed down from his perch. Simon was on the roof and quickly joined him as Jeremy came to a halt.

"Sir, I have a message from—"

Marcus raised a hand, cutting him off, not wanting anyone to hear the name and give away where Chapon's family was hidden. He took the folded page and opened it, smiling at the single word. He turned to his sergeant. "It's time."

Simon grunted. "Thank God. I was meant to swing a sword, not a hammer." He lowered his voice. "But what of the renter?"

Marcus chewed his cheek for a moment, coming to a decision and turning to Jeremy. "Do you know where the clothing shop is that Mr. Chapon referred to?"

"I do. I got directions from him before I left."

"Good. I want you to watch the shop and see if anyone comes in around closing that looks suspicious. The owner claims that the basement was being rented by someone else, and that he had no idea what was going on there."

"And should someone arrive?"

"Follow him and see where he goes, then return to Sir Denys' and wait for me."

"Understood." Jeremy headed toward the shop on his horse, and Marcus beckoned Richart over.

"I'm afraid we must leave for now. Can you finish this on your own?"

"Absolutely, sir. We'll have this house buttoned up before sun falls, or I'll be here until the wee hours of the morning finishing it myself."

Marcus smiled, putting a hand on the man's shoulder. "You are a good man, sir. You and your family will be in my prayers tonight."

Richart smiled and bowed. "Thank you, sir. You honor me."

Marcus mounted his horse and he and Simon left the construction scene behind, his thoughts on Thomas, and whether the young man was even alive to enjoy the fruits of his neighbors' labor.

Please, Lord, let this all have not been in vain.

Palais de la Cité
Paris, Kingdom of France

Denys doubled over, the pain in his stomach crippling, his entire body twisted in pain. Benuche, standing nearby, stepped over quickly and grabbed him by the arms, leading him from the Court before too many took notice of what was occurring. Once they were in the hallway, he leaned him against the wall.

"This is the worst I've ever seen it."

"You knew this could happen?"

"Yes, it's rare that it happens so quickly, though I have heard tell of it. When I was in the Holy Land, I visited what they called an opium den, and saw people in horrific shape outside who couldn't afford to indulge. The proprietor said everyone was different, some not developing any dependency, others developing it after only a couple of tries."

"You knew this, yet you let me take this? I thought we were friends."

"I never imagined someone such as yourself could be so afflicted. You are a strong, healthy man who enjoys the good life. Your indulgences are legendary among the Court. I would never have imagined that your body would prove so weak."

Denys was about to object to the word choice when he heaved his lunch onto the marble floor. Several servants rushed over, quickly forming a human shield, their backs turned to him to provide some semblance of privacy in his weakened state.

"Arrange a private room for us."

"At once, sir."

"And send for my man. Tell him to bring my kit."

"Yes, sir."

Two of the staff rushed away to execute Benuche's orders while he and the others helped Denys toward the private rooms where he could rest. In short order, he was sequestered from the public eye and lying on a bed as comfortable as any in the Kingdom. He curled into a ball, drawing his knees up to his chest as his entire body shook.

There was a knock at the door and Benuche opened it, his man entering, handing him a bundle. Denys recognized what was inside the moment the first item was unpacked. The opium lamp was lit, the bowl placed overtop the flame, a ball of the black paste dropped inside the water it contained. The pipe was fit in place in preparation for the sweet relief that would soon be available to any who chose to draw upon it.

He shook his head. "No, I cannot."

"You'll die if you don't."

The suggestion terrified him. "What do you mean?"

"People have been known to die from the withdrawal. You must take this."

He once again shook his head, his duty to Marcus and the others front of mind.

"Just take it. You won't need a lot, and then you can wean yourself off it slowly. I've seen it done before. And to be frank, after seeing its effects on you, I too intend to stop. No amount of pleasure is worth such pain."

"But I mustn't, I must be ready."

"Ready for what?"

His pain was clouding his mind. He couldn't speak of what was going on.

"Please, Sir Denys, save yourself. Just one draw. That might be all you need."

He thought of this morning and how he'd been able to function quite well after several draws on the pipe. Could one draw really hurt? He acquiesced, and Benuche handed him the pipe with the water in the bowl now boiling, signaling the sweet relief he desperately needed was at hand.

161

De Montfort Estate
Paris, Kingdom of France

Marcus stepped into the sitting room at Denys' estate, finding David, Isabelle, Thibault, and Enzo waiting for him.

His squire sprang to his feet. "Should I remove your armor, sir?"

Marcus shook his head. "No. We'll be departing shortly." He turned to one of the servants. "Can you please bring the marshal?"

"Right away, sir." The man disappeared.

"Where's Jeremy?" asked David.

"I have him watching the clothing shop. The proprietor claims ignorance. He says someone is renting the basement and is due to pay his weekly rent at close of business today. I have Jeremy watching in case the man arrives."

"Do you really think he might? It would be rather foolish, wouldn't it?"

Marcus sat on the edge of a chair. "You forget one thing: What this person is doing isn't illegal."

"Attempting to kill us wasn't?"

"There's no way we can prove he was involved. He can merely claim that it was locals, jealous of Thomas' new-found success. We have nothing that would link him to the attack on the residence."

"But they closed their business last night, didn't they? They fled the area."

"They did, but that could be merely temporary. He

might continue to rent the place, then return in several days or weeks once he feels it's safe to do so."

David's head bobbed slowly. "Yes, I suppose that's possible. And what of Sir Denys' message? I assume it means that Prince Louis is in court?"

"That's what I take it to mean, as well. Simon and I will attempt to follow the Prince and see if he goes anywhere but his home."

"And myself?"

"You'll accompany us, and once we have a location, you'll return here and direct Sir Denys' guard so they can join us."

"Understood."

There was a rap at the door then it opened, the marshal entering. Marcus rose. "Marshal Guillaume, my sergeant and I will be leaving shortly with my squire. Once we have a location, my squire will return to direct you. Will your men be ready?"

"They will be, sir. However, we cannot leave without a direct order from Sir Denys."

Marcus nodded. "Of course. Your master should have returned from court before my squire arrives."

"Yes, sir. Do you expect a fight?"

"I expect that when we arrive in numbers, they will surrender without opposition. We will retrieve Thomas, then get to the bottom of what is truly going on."

"Very good, sir." Guillaume bowed and left the room, closing the door behind him.

Simon entered, fresh from having relieved himself. He dropped in a chair, sighing. "You have no idea how much I needed that." Marcus and David chuckled, and Thibault rolled her eyes.

Isabelle stared blankly. "What did you need?"

Marcus waved a hand, dismissing her question. "Trust me, you don't want to understand most of what comes out of my uncouth sergeant's mouth."

Her blank stare turned into one of realization, then shock. "Really, Simon? Must you?"

He grinned. "It's in my nature, miss."

"You clearly were raised among men."

Simon shrugged. "This is true, though I can't complain. While the stench may be far worse, there is less drama."

Thibault regarded him. "It's drama that makes life worth living."

164

Outside the Clothing Shop
Paris, Kingdom of France

Jeremy stood in an alleyway across from the clothing shop, stamping his feet and rubbing his hands together in the chill. He pressed his body against his horse, drawing from her body heat, wishing he could start a fire. As the man on the bottom rung of the ladder of their four-man team, he was accustomed to the shit assignments, and it didn't really bother him. In fact, it didn't bother him at all. He would lay down his life for Marcus, without hesitation. He would even lay it down for that bastard David, who, though he teased him incessantly, was the best friend he had in the world.

And besides, anything beat shoveling shit all day.

He smiled at the image of Thomas doing just that, and prayed they found the young man alive, not only for the boy's sake, but for his own, so a fifth, lower rung would be added to the ladder. A new low-man on the ladder meant his shit shoveling days were, at least partially, over. If Thomas and Isabelle did indeed split their time between the city and the farm, he would still be shoveling in the winter months, though that task was far less unpleasant in the chill of winter, than the heat of summer.

A young woman stepped from the shop, accompanied by a much older man, and they climbed into their carriage, an intricate coat of arms nailed to its side. It pulled away as the shopkeeper stepped outside, removing the torches on either side of the door, signaling he was closed for the day.

Jeremy stood upright as this was the appointed hour, should the renter decide to continue to pay. He stood, staring at the door, and the longer he did so, the more he feared blinking lest he miss something. His eyes burned, and he was forced to blink several times, then breathed a little easier as he realized he had been foolish in his unwarranted concern.

He heard a horse approaching and was tempted to poke his head out from the alley to see who was coming, but resisted the urge. He couldn't risk being spotted. Here in the shadows, in the fading light, he would go unnoticed. The horse came to a halt in front of the shop and a man dismounted. He knocked on the door and it was opened a moment later, as if the proprietor were expecting him.

This must be the renter.

Jeremy cocked an ear in an attempt to hear any conversation, but the man was received in silence. He stepped inside and the door closed. Jeremy mounted his horse, patting her neck gently to silence the excited beast as she responded to his own change of mood. The door opened several minutes later and the man stepped out, mounting his horse and departing in the same direction from which he came. Jeremy gently urged his horse forward and followed the man through the streets, his heart pounding with excitement and fear.

As they continued, he attempted to guess what their ultimate destination might be, and as the pursuit persisted, his stomach became knots as he realized they were heading directly for the Templar Fortress that was the headquarters of the Order in the Kingdom of France.

Could Templars indeed be involved? And if they

were, was it sanctioned? If the man was heading to the Fortress, it had to mean he was a Templar in good standing, not one who had been dismissed from the Order in disgrace.

They turned a corner and Jeremy gulped at the sight of the massive complex ahead of them, one that rivaled any in Christendom. With each step his horse took, drawing them ever closer to the Templar sanctuary, his heart sank further, and when the man he was pursuing hailed the guards standing at the front gate, and they returned it with friendly waves, he finally knew the truth.

His order was indeed behind the kidnapping, and perhaps murder, of Thomas, the attempted murder of the Chapon family and Isabelle, and the provision of the sinful opium to the unsuspecting masses.

And for the first time in his life, he was ashamed to be associated with the Templars.

Outside Palais de la Cité
Paris, Kingdom of France

Marcus stood next to his horse, Simon beside him. They had both removed their Templar surcoats and were wearing plain black ones provided by the staff at Denys' estate. The animosity between King Phillip's family and the Templar Order was well-known. The King had borrowed heavily to fund his military campaigns against England, and was struggling to make the payments required to the Order. It was an embarrassment for the King, and a constant thorn in the man's side, that he, anointed by God himself, could owe such a sum to an organization that had its members take a vow of poverty.

Marcus himself was sometimes in awe of how wealthy the Templar Order was. Many jealous souls assumed they profited from ill-gotten gains, however that wasn't the case at all. Yes, sometimes the Order received a share of the spoils from a successful battle, however the vast majority of their income came from their financial network. Thousands upon thousands used their encoded letters of credit to safely transfer their money from wherever they might be in Europe, to the Holy Land, and back again, all for a fee. They would deposit whatever wealth it was here, the value would be itemized and written on a letter of credit in code, then that letter would be given to the pilgrim or nobleman who would then present it once they arrived in the Holy Land, where an equivalent amount would be returned, minus the fee.

This had made the Order extremely wealthy, to the point where it needed to divest itself of the tremendous amount of gold and silver and other items of value it held in its vaults. The Templar Order was the largest holder of real estate in all of Christendom, owned fleets of ships, untold numbers of businesses, and was an economic powerhouse, all sanctioned by the Pope, and protected by the Roman Catholic Church. No king dared challenge them, and it enraged King Phillip The Fair, whose title had nothing to do with how he dispensed justice, and everything to do with how he perceived his looks.

Simon held up the cushion cover, brought in case they didn't recognize the coat of arms, and pointed at a carriage leaving the rear gate of the palace. "Is that it?"

Marcus squinted in the dim light. "It is."

Simon stuffed the cushion back in his saddlebags and they all mounted their horses, following the carriage at a safe distance. In less than half an hour, they were at the Prince's estate, the coat of arms proudly displayed on stone gateposts.

Simon cursed. "Well, this was a waste of time."

"You didn't expect him to actually go there directly after court, did you?"

"I did. I figured he was as pig of a man as his brother."

"I have no doubt he's every bit as immoral a character as the King, however even he likely has his limitations."

"So, what do we do?"

"We wait. If he was set up with a private corner to inhale his opium, then I have no doubt he has become dependent upon it, just as Sir Denys has. He will be

169

expecting to use it this evening."

"But Sir Denys had it brought to his house, so why wouldn't the Prince?"

"I'm not sure why he wouldn't, however it was obvious he hadn't. If he had, we wouldn't have found his private corner in the opium lounge, now would we?"

Simon grunted. "I'll leave the thinking to you."

"A wise choice," snickered David.

Simon gave him a withering look. "I'd watch my tongue if I were you."

David stuck it out, staring down. "Odd, I can't seem to do that. Can you?"

Marcus chuckled as he guided them down the road, finding no alleyways here in which to hide. "David, make a circuit of the property. Make sure there are no rear entrances that we're not seeing."

"Yes, sir."

David rode off as Marcus and Simon dismounted. "How long do you think we'll be here?"

"I suspect hours, unfortunately."

"Lovely. I need to piss again."

Marcus eyed his friend. "You've been doing that a lot lately."

"I've been thirsty, so I've been drinking more water than I'm accustomed to. I guess I'm getting old."

Marcus backhanded the man on the shoulder. "Don't speak like that. If you're getting old, then I'm getting even older, and I've got three young children to raise."

"Then I guess you should've kept it in your pants."

Marcus laughed. "That sword has been sheathed

since the day I was born, and will remain so until the day I die."

"The world's loss, I'm sure. Do you ever wonder what it's like?"

"Of course I do, from time to time. What man wouldn't? Though, when I feel the urge to explore those thoughts, I pray, and the urges are soon forgotten. Yourself?"

"All the bloody time now that I'm living on that farm. One advantage of being in the Order is that you're surrounded by nothing but sagging balls. Now, we have Lady Joanne, Beatrice, and Isabelle surrounding us day in and day out, and I can't help but notice that I have an attraction for all of them."

Marcus regarded his friend. "Then why not act upon it?"

"Excuse me?"

"I don't mean an illicit relationship. I mean, if you have such desires, then leave the Order. No one would think any less of you. The four of us are barely in the Order now, as it is. Leave the Order with no shame, stay on the farm with us, take a wife. You deserve it, if you think it would make you happy."

Simon stared at him. "Did you sample some of that opium without me knowing?"

Marcus laughed. "I'm being serious."

"As am I. It was a daft idea when it was floated to you last year, as it is now. Isabelle would've married you in a heartbeat. We even told you to do so and you refused, instead choosing to remain with the Order, your vows intact. And I choose to do the same."

"Then the matter is settled. We will speak of your little sword no more."

"I'd appreciate that."

Outside the Enclos du Temple, Templar Fortress
Paris, Kingdom of France

Jeremy sat on his horse, just down the road from the entrance to the Templar Fortress, each flap of the Order's flag overhead stinging as if it were a whip to his soul with the knowledge he now possessed. He couldn't go inside, for he didn't know who he could trust. He couldn't believe that all of his brothers were involved, yet at least some were. And for the man to so brazenly enter without the markings of the Order, the corruption had to go either to the top, or very close to it.

He was sick to his stomach at the thought. He had met Sir Matthew Norris, the head of the Order in the Kingdom of France, and thought him a good man. He couldn't believe that he would be involved in such a sinful endeavor. Yet his grand sum of exposure to the man was under an hour in his entire life, and could one really know someone in an hour?

He wasn't certain what to do. This information was of critical importance to Marcus, yet didn't he also need to know the man's ultimate destination? But what if the man remained inside the Fortress all night?

He stared at the flag, rustling in the wind, then made his decision, urging his horse forward, and praying the choice he had just made was the correct one.

Unknown Location

Thomas woke to someone smacking his cheek. He groaned as his eyes fluttered open. The combination of the opium, lack of food, and insufficient sleep, had him as groggy as he had ever felt.

"Good, you're alive."

He looked up at the man leaning over him. This was the first time he had seen him as more than a shadow. His vision was blurred, though he couldn't say he recognized the man from the neighborhood.

His pulse pounded at the implications.

Until this point, he hadn't seen any faces, he had only heard voices. But now this one face, this key face, had been revealed to him, and it could mean only one thing.

They had decided he was to die.

After being moved from what he assumed was the basement under the clothing shop, a move that appeared to be executed in a panic, he had been held in this room in an unknown location. All he was aware of was that it took far less than half an hour to arrive here by the carriage he had been thrown into the back of, the drawn curtains preventing him from knowing anything other than the fact they had crossed the Seine River, the distinctive sound of traveling over a bridge and the familiar smell of the water tipping him off. But from there, for the life of him, he had no clue where they went.

"Friends of yours will be arriving shortly to deal with you."

174

A slight surge of hope rushed through him at the choice of words.

"Rather, I should say, friends of your friends."

He frowned. He had few friends, few he could trust. He had none in the neighborhood that he had called home most of his life. They would likely rejoice at his situation, their jealousy intense. The thought had him reconsidering the decision come to by him and Isabelle. Could he put her through that? Could he put her through the stares, the glares, the snide remarks, the petty jealousies for half of each year, for half her remaining life?

It didn't bother him that much, though deep down, it probably did. He preferred to be alone, but that wasn't her. She thrived on being the center of attention, of talking to anyone and everyone about everything. It was a rare moment indeed when her mouth wasn't in motion.

It was one of the things he loved about her. She was just so full of life, and he wondered if his neighborhood, filled with animosity and suffering, would drum that spirit out of her.

Another slap. "Are you still with me, boy?"

Thomas leaned away from what he feared would be yet another smack to his face. "To what friends do you refer?"

"Your Templar friends, of course."

Thomas' eyes narrowed. "You mean Sir Marcus and Simon?"

"They are your friends, are they not?"

"Yes. Are they coming?"

The man laughed. "My dear boy, they have no inkling of where you are. However, since all Templars are brothers, and most brothers are friends, then those that are arriving here shortly, to put an end to my troubles, must be friends of this Sir Marcus you hold in such high esteem."

"What are they going to do with me?"

The man smiled broadly. "Why, kill you, of course."

Thomas was too weak to protest, and instead merely slumped in the corner in which he sat. The man kicked him, but Thomas ignored him, not willing to give him the satisfaction of a response. He instead feigned sleep and the man growled, storming away and up a set of stairs that lay beyond a door to his left.

Thomas opened his eyes, concentrating hard as he attempted to cut through the fog of his brain. An opium pipe lay on his chest, the lamp and bowl beside him bubbling away, the flame flickering gently. He couldn't remember the last time he had inhaled, and he had no intention of doing so now, though if someone were to enter the room, he had at least to feign his continued use of the vile substance.

He repositioned the pipe so the vapors wafting out of the end of it wouldn't be accidentally inhaled, then looked about the room, the only light from the lamp and a lone candle near the door. It appeared to be another basement, this one in reasonable shape, though too small to be a replacement to their setup he had been held in earlier.

He could hear activity on the other side of the wall, several men speaking. He strained to hear their words, but could only make out the occasional one, though he was left with the impression they were hastily recreating the basement that had just been abandoned, no doubt readying themselves for clientele that were due to arrive shortly.

Wherever they were, his captors felt secure enough to set up business, at least temporarily. And that meant they would need to inform their patrons where to go. And it left him wondering if Chapon would be included on the invite list. If he were, and Enzo was to think of it, there might be some faint hope of someone finding him.

Yet none of that would matter if he were dead upon their arrival.

He had to escape himself.

He stared at the door. He had heard a lock engaged when his captor left, and there were stairs on the opposite side. Wherever he was couldn't be that large. In fact, the wall he leaned against was cold, which meant it was an outer wall. It might be as simple as going through the door, up the stairs, then out another door.

If he could somehow get past the lock.

The thought had him struggling to his feet.

And it was at that moment he realized how difficult any flight would be. This was the first time he had stood in at least a day, perhaps more, and in his weakened state, if he were pursued, he would have no hope of escaping. His only hope would be to draw the attention of passers-by, though depending upon the hour, those might be few and far between.

He took a tentative step toward the door. The sound of a metal chain dragging had him staring down at his own feet, all hope swiftly fleeing his body at the sight of the irons clasped to his left leg, a long chain leading under the door where it was secured out of sight and out of reach. He dropped back into his corner, his shoulders heaving as tears flowed down his cheeks, and he silently apologized to Isabelle for the future they would never share.

De Montfort Estate
Paris, Kingdom of France

Jeremy rushed into the sitting room, finding Isabelle, Thibault, and Enzo. "Where is Sir Marcus?"

"He, Simon, and David left to follow Prince Louis," replied Isabelle.

"When did they leave?"

"Several hours ago. Why? Do you have news?"

"I do."

Thibault frowned. "Judging from the expression on your face, boy, I suspect it's grim."

"It is, indeed. I watched the clothing shop as Sir Marcus ordered, and shortly after it closed, a man arrived on horseback. He went inside for a few moments, then left. I assumed him to be the renter that was expected at that hour, so I followed him." His voice drifted off as he searched for the words he couldn't believe needed to be spoken.

"Well, out with it, boy. We haven't got all day!"

He flinched at Thibault's snapped words. He inhaled some courage. "I followed him to the Templar Fortress."

Everyone, including Enzo, gasped at the revelation.

"But that can't be!" cried Isabelle. "That means Templars *are* involved!"

Jeremy nodded. "I can see no other conclusion."

"Was he wearing any Templar markings?" asked Thibault.

"None that I saw, though when he arrived, he was

greeted at the gate as if he were familiar to the guards."

"Then it would appear Sir Marcus was wise not to inform the Fortress."

Isabelle's hands wrung in her lap. "What are we going to do? Who can we trust if not the Templars?"

Jeremy collapsed into a chair, the energy surging through his veins that had kept him going, now betraying him. "I don't know what to do. Sir Marcus has to be informed that he cannot trust our order."

"Do you think it's all of them?"

Jeremy vigorously shook his head. "Never! Any of those I have served with over the years would absolutely refuse to participate. It must be a few, however we have no way of knowing if they are the lowest of the low or the highest of the high. For all we know, Sir Matthew could be behind it."

"Who's that?" asked Isabelle.

"He's the head of our order in the Kingdom of France. I've met him. I always thought him a good man, though now I wonder."

Thibault's finger tapped rapidly on the arm of her chair, then it stopped. "Don't be so quick to judge. In my experience, much can happen under the nose of those in charge when the numbers are great. I've seen the comings and goings of that fortress, and there are so many of you, I find it highly unlikely Sir Matthew knows half of what goes on within the walls he commands. He should be informed."

"But can we take that risk? Can we ask him for assistance, ask him to root out those behind this?"

Thibault frowned. "In such instances, I find it's best to go with one's gut."

Jeremy regarded her. "And what does your gut tell

you?"

"What mine tells me is of no consequence. I know none of the parties involved. You know your order, you've met Sir Matthew. It's your gut that should be listened to, not mine."

Jeremy frowned, his stomach churning with the responsibility. He sighed. "I'm afraid mine tells me nothing beyond it having the need to vomit. All I do know is that I must inform Sir Marcus that Templars are indeed involved, and that he must be careful should any arrive."

"And just how do you propose to find him? All we know is that he was at the King's Court, and has likely left by now, following Prince Louis."

Jeremy thought for a moment. "Well, if he is following Prince Louis, where is the man most likely to have gone after court?"

"Home?" suggested Enzo.

Jeremy agreed. "That's what I would think as well. I can't see any other choice but to go there."

"There is another thing to consider," said Thibault.

"What's that?"

"These men, with their attempt on all of our lives, have shown they are willing to kill. If they are indeed Templars, then we must expect that their guard will be up, and they will be waiting for any attempt to rescue Thomas should he still be alive."

Isabelle yelped in horror, clasping both hands over her mouth to silence her brief scream. Thibault patted the girl on her leg, and Enzo leaned slightly closer. "You mean they could be walking into a trap?"

Thibault nodded. "They could be. The plan, as I understand it, was they were to find out where this opium lounge had been moved to, then send word here for Sir Denys' men to be called upon to assist in the rescue. I've seen no sign of Sir Denys, and his marshal has indicated he will not go without the personal command of his master."

Jeremy suppressed a curse. "So, Sir Marcus and Simon could be there alone?"

"Exactly."

He rose. "Then that makes it doubly important I warn them."

"Yes, however, again, you could be chasing shadows, as we have no idea where they actually are. Yet there is one action you could take that may save them all."

Jeremy stared at her. "What?"

"Speak with Sir Matthew."

Jeremy collapsed back in his chair, the very thought terrifying. He could be going into the lion's den, only to be mauled by the head of the pride sitting behind a desk, wearing the markings of the order to which he had devoted his life. It could mean certain death.

And the very notion had him gripped with fear.

"You seem to be having trouble coming to a decision."

He reluctantly nodded.

"I suspect it has something to do with the fact that your order is involved, and not a lack of courage. I've seen you fight, and you are no coward."

He inhaled quickly, his chest expanding as he sat upright. "You're right, I'm being foolish about this. If it were any other place, I wouldn't hesitate. Just because it's the Templar Fortress doesn't make the urgency any less. If I should die, then I die. But if I succeed, Sir Matthew may be able to determine who among the Order have been corrupted, force them to reveal the new location, then send help." He rose. "Word should still be sent to Sir Marcus, however. If there's even the slightest chance he's at Prince Louis' estate, we must attempt to inform him of what may lie ahead so that he can save himself."

Thibault regarded him. "Knowing Sir Marcus, he wouldn't change his plans regardless of the news."

"He might be more cautious."

"Have you ever known him not to be?"

"No, I suppose not."

"Then I think you know your answer. Sending a messenger at this hour to search the area surrounding Prince Louis' estate may raise suspicions, and bring about the very result you fear."

His shoulders slumped. "You're right, of course."

Thibault smiled. "I always am."

Outside Price Louis' Estate
Paris, Kingdom of France

Marcus spotted David riding down the road in front of Prince Louis' massive estate. He executed a bird call and David rode toward them then dismounted.

"Report."

"The estate backs onto the river. He could leave by boat if he so desired, however it would mean he would require horses unless his destination was on the water."

Marcus shook his head. "I doubt that would be the case. Let's assume he'll be traveling by horse and carriage. What about side exits?"

"There are estates on either side, both walled as this one is. It would appear that the only way in or out of anything along this road is by boat at the rear or through the front gates."

"Excellent. That makes our job much easier. Now we just have to hope that this entire venture wasn't a waste of time, and that he does indeed leave here to go where we hope he will be going."

Simon pointed to the gate. "I don't know where he's going, though he is going somewhere."

The gate swung open and two guards on horseback emerged, followed by a carriage, the Prince's personal coat of arms on the side, then two more guards on horses. The gate closed and the entourage turned to the right, heading toward the less affluent part of the city, though judging from what Marcus could see from here, that would be all parts of the Kingdom. Marcus mounted his horse, as did the others, and began the pursuit, staying at a safe distance, the pace set by those they followed, leisurely at best. It appeared they were in no hurry, and were more concerned with giving the Prince a comfortable ride.

He turned in his saddle toward David. "When we arrive at our final destination, you'll have to remember how to get there, so pay attention for landmarks and how to get back to Sir Denys'. Minutes may be of importance."

"You can count on me, sir."

"I know I can. When you arrive, have Sir Denys bring his men in the greatest numbers possible, and have Jeremy join you."

"And Tanya?"

Marcus chuckled. "As good as she is in a fight, tonight we will require the element of surprise, and a barking dog is no way to achieve that."

David agreed. "Good thinking."

Approaching the Enclos du Temple, Templar Fortress
Paris, Kingdom of France

Jeremy approached the Templar Fortress, his terrified self soaked in sweat. He had been here several times since circumstances had brought them to France, yet he never ceased to be amazed at how imposing a structure it was. It was a massive walled complex with guards dotting the towers, the colors proudly displayed in the center of a kingdom ruled by a man who despised them. It was a bold statement that none should dare touch them, their power and wealth so great that even the will of kings bowed before their authority.

He had always been proud to be a Templar, despite pride being a sin. He believed in what they stood for, he believed in their purpose. Knights were sworn to protect the weak, the poor, those who couldn't help themselves. And the Templars were the greatest order of knights the world had ever known. Tens of thousands of men with a single purpose—to protect the innocent from the evil that filled the world.

He drew a breath and held it as he approached the gates. A guard hailed him with a smile, recognizing the brown surcoat with cross marking him as a squire of the Order. "What brings you here today, squire, without your master?"

"I have urgent business to discuss with Sir Matthew Norris, on behalf of Sir Marcus de Rancourt."

"Do you know where to go?"

"I do."

The man waved him through. "Then good luck in

seeing him. He's not one to often meet with squires."

"Let's hope today is a rare day."

The man laughed. "For your sake, I hope it is."

Jeremy continued inside, his heart hammering as he struggled to regain control. Fear wasn't the enemy, letting the fear dominate one's senses was. A hammering heart, pounding ears, and jittery hands could get one killed, though fear itself could also heighten the senses, allowing one to detect an enemy all the more easier.

Yet only if it were controlled.

He inhaled again and held the breath, counting in his head before slowly exhaling, repeating the process several times as he approached the main entrance to the headquarters. A stable boy rushed up and grabbed the reins of his horse as he dismounted. "Greetings, squire. Whom do you serve?"

"Sir Marcus de Rancourt."

The young boy's eyes widened with delight as he stared up at Jeremy. "Did he mention me? Quentin? I helped him a few weeks ago."

Jeremy stared at him for a moment, unsure of anything, when he finally remembered the name. "Of course, of course. How are you?"

"I am well, thank you. How can I take care of your horse? Will you be here long?"

"No, I expect I could be leaving in minutes. She's been well-tended, so just give her some water and feed, but don't remove the saddle. If there's time, brush her down. I'm not sure how long I will be, but I will likely be leaving in a hurry."

"I'll take good care of her."

He led the horse away, and Jeremy frowned as he realized it might be his only means of escape.

He stepped through the massive doors and into a large room, chairs lining the walls, some occupied by those waiting for an audience. He stepped up to the sergeant manning the desk at the center of the room and bowed deeply.

"I have urgent business with Sir Matthew Norris."

The sergeant looked up from a document he was reading, his eyes widening slightly at the sight of a squire. "Do you now?" He leaned back, folding his arms. "And just what might that business be?"

"Business that can only be discussed with Sir Matthew."

"And where is your master?"

"His life is in danger. It's urgent that I speak to Sir Matthew on his behalf."

"And just who is your master?"

"Sir Marcus de Rancourt."

One eyebrow shot up. "Sir Marcus? I know him. I served with his sergeant, Simon Chastain, in the Holy Land." He regarded Jeremy. "And you're one of his squires. I recognize you. Which one are you? David or Jeremy?"

An audible sigh escaped Jeremy as he realized he might be in the company of a friend. "I'm Jeremy."

"Do you not recognize me? Sergeant Paumier?"

Jeremy shook his head. "I'm afraid not, Sergeant. As squires, we're taught not to stare at those above us in rank."

"True." Paumier visibly relaxed. "How is that crusty old bastard, Simon?"

Jeremy smiled. "As crusty as ever."

"So, you said your master's life is in danger?"

"Yes, as is Simon's. It's urgent I speak to Sir Matthew immediately."

"I'll see what I can do." Paumier pointed at one of the chairs. "Have a seat."

Jeremy bowed then retreated to one of the seats, sitting as Paumier left the room. He said a silent prayer as he glanced around at the others, many looking bored, many tired, and all appearing as if they had been there for some time.

The door Paumier had departed through opened, and the sergeant beckoned him. Jeremy grinned and leaped to his feet, rushing toward the door, several of the others audibly muttering in protest that he had received an audience so quickly. Within moments, he was standing in front of Sir Matthew Norris. Jeremy bowed deeply, holding it until he was acknowledged.

"Your name is Jeremy?"

"Yes. We've met before, though briefly. I'm sure you wouldn't remember me. I am a squire to Sir Marcus de Rancourt."

Matthew assessed him, his eyes narrowing. "Yes, I recall, the squire who can't control his emotions."

Jeremy stared at his feet, suddenly uncomfortable. "I was hoping you wouldn't remember that."

Matthew ignored his comment. "My sergeant tells me that your master's life is in danger."

"Yes." Jeremy glanced about to make sure they were alone, the door closing as Paumier returned to his post. "I fear I have news that you will find troubling, and perhaps impossible to believe."

Matthew leaned back and folded his arms. "Enlighten me."

Jeremy quickly filled him in on the details of what had brought them all to Paris, then the information that the baker had provided suggesting Templars were supplying the opium.

Matthew interrupted him. "Wait a moment. You're suggesting that members of our order are bringing opium into Paris?"

"Yes, sir. That's what the baker overheard."

Matthew firmly shook his head, and the offense he was taking had Jeremy believing that if the conspiracy were indeed true, Matthew knew nothing of it. "Do you have any further evidence beyond the word of this baker?"

"Unfortunately, I do, sir."

Matthew leaned forward. "Well, out with it. What is this evidence?"

"On Sir Marcus' order, I watched the location where this opium operation was run out of until only last night. The shop owner had claimed ignorance, stating he was renting out the basement, and that the man would be coming tonight at close of business to pay his weekly rent. I watched, and a man did indeed arrive immediately after closing. He was only in the shop for a few minutes, so I assumed that he was the renter that I had been sent to follow. I followed him, and…" He hesitated.

"And what?"

"And he came here, sir. He came through the gates, was greeted by the guards as if they knew him well, and rode inside despite wearing none of our colors."

Matthew's jaw dropped and he collapsed back in his

chair. "I find this impossible to believe."

"I swear to you, sir, I'm not lying."

Matthew shook a hand in front of him. "No, no, that's not what I meant. I believe you, but there must be some sort of reasonable explanation. I find it impossible to believe that our brothers could be involved."

"Nor did I, sir, until a short while ago when this man came here."

"How long ago was it?"

"No more than a couple of hours."

Matthew rose. "And where is Sir Marcus now?"

"He's attempting to find their new location by following Prince Louis, who we believe is a user of this opium."

Matthew cursed. "If a member of our order is caught interfering in the affairs of the brother of a king who has made no secret of the fact he hates us, it could spell trouble for the Order. We must stop him."

"There's no way to, sir. We have no idea where the Prince is going."

"There is one way."

"What's that, sir?"

"We find out who is involved, and make them tell us where your master may be heading."

Jeremy smiled. "I like the way you think, sir."

Outer edge of the slums
Paris, Kingdom of France

Marcus stared from their hiding place at the building just down the road. There was nothing special about it, though it was in a much better neighborhood than the previous location of the opium lounge. If this indeed was their new site, it would appear they were moving up in the world. Travel from Prince Louis' estate to the clothing shop in the slums took almost half an hour, whereas the journey here was less than half that. If they hoped to upgrade their clientele from bakers to princes, then this was the way to do it. The carriage was parked out front, the Prince clearly having no concerns about his presence there being noticed. His personal guard of four remained outside, and appeared more concerned with the chill in the air than defending against any threats.

"Do you see anyone else?"

Simon shook his head. "No, just the four of them plus the coachman. It would appear those running the operation have no concerns for security that I can see."

David looked at them. "Are we sure that this is the new location? Perhaps this is an innocent visit to a friend."

Marcus disagreed. "Princes don't visit friends in neighborhoods such as this."

"A woman perhaps?"

"He would have had arrangements made, then met her someplace he could flaunt his wealth."

"Well, with that carriage, he's certainly flaunting it here."

"True, but we must remember that nothing of what is going on here is a crime, though it is a sin in my books. The Prince is free to partake in the opium, and these men are free to provide it. What *is* a crime is the kidnapping of Thomas and the attempted murder of Isabelle and the Chapon family."

"I've been thinking about that," said Simon.

"Always dangerous," interjected David.

Simon lunged out with his chin then snapped his teeth like a dog. David flinched and Simon smiled with satisfaction. "As I was saying, I was thinking about that. Why kidnap Thomas in the first place? Why go to all this trouble if they're doing nothing wrong?"

"I've been thinking about that as well," said Marcus.

"And have you come to any conclusions that my feeble brain hasn't been able to conceive of?"

"The only thing I can think of is that if Templars are providing the opium, that would go against the laws we live by, and if Sir Matthew were to find out, he would swiftly put an end to it, cutting off their supply. Thomas was probably grabbed because he was caught sneaking around. They interrogated him, found out his connection to us, and decided they couldn't let him go because he might tell us what had happened, and we might then look into things."

"So, what you're saying is if we weren't his friends, he'd probably be alive and well today."

Marcus frowned. "I wasn't thinking of it in those terms, though I do believe you're correct. We might be indirectly responsible for anything that has happened to him." He turned to David. "I'm convinced this is the

193

location. Go get Sir Denys' personal guard."

"Yes, sir." David leaped onto the back of his horse, Marcus' squire of so many years charging off into the dark to fetch the help they would need.

Simon patted his horse's neck, the beast shifting as if eager to join in the gallop. "So, now what do we do?"

"We wait."

Simon grunted. "Something we seem to be doing a lot of lately."

"True. It would be more comfortable if this were happening at the height of summer."

Simon grinned. "If you'd like, I can go ask them to reschedule the kidnapping."

Marcus chuckled. "If you think it would work."

Simon became serious. "So, what of Thomas and Isabelle? Do you think this plan of theirs will work?"

Marcus sighed heavily. "I'm not sure, though I think it's the only hope they have. I had thought that Isabelle would have no hope of enjoying life in the city after hearing Thomas speak of his neighbors, however after what I saw today with everyone pulling together to rebuild his home, there is clearly love there that he is unaware of. He should take this opportunity to reembrace his community. Because of his work, he has far more money than most of them, and perhaps he can put some of that to good use."

"I fear the goodwill may not last," said Simon. "The moment Enzo breaks somebody's hand because of a late payment, all eyes will turn to Thomas."

Marcus had to agree with his sergeant's assessment. As long as Thomas worked for Thibault, his life would be difficult if he chose to stay in his family's home. "I wonder if he would be willing to relocate."

"He already said he hates the farm."

"No, I mean within the city, perhaps to a neighborhood such as this."

"Do you think he'd be able to afford such a thing?"

"If he committed to working for Mrs. Thibault, he could afford something on the outskirts, still within the slums, though not in the epicenter as he is now. It would take him away from most of the clientele that he deals with, and his neighbors would have no need to know what he did. It might make life easier."

Simon chewed his cheek for a moment as he stared at the houses around them. "Knowing him and Isabelle, I can't possibly see them fitting into a neighborhood such as this. I suspect it is filled with people desperate to be part of high society, who would treat a poor boy from the slums and a simple girl from the farm quite terribly."

Marcus frowned. "I hadn't thought of that, but I'm afraid you may be right."

"See, I'm not all brawn and good looks."

Marcus eyed him. "You do have your moments. Try not to waste them all at once."

"I wonder if there's some way that Thomas could put that mind of his to work in some other manner."

"The only thing I can think of is to work for the King, and I fear if he were to find out that Thomas is an acquaintance of ours, it would put an end to any such notion."

Simon sighed. "Then it truly does appear Thomas is trapped between a life working for a criminal, or toiling on a farm."

"Agreed. And that would mean he would come to resent Isabelle, and both their lives would be ruined."

Simon folded his arms, shaking his head. "You do realize this is all your fault?"

"What do you mean?"

"If you had just married Isabelle like she wanted, she'd be happy for the rest of her life living on the farm, and Thomas would never have caught her eye."

Marcus groaned. "Rid yourself of that notion. She would have quickly tired of me then have been miserable. I think we should see how their solution plays out. If the neighbors embrace her, she could be quite happy here, and perhaps in time, Thomas could learn to enjoy life on the farm."

"The only way that's going to happen is if Jeremy starts shoveling the shit again."

Marcus chuckled. "Yes, I suppose I shouldn't have let the squires assign his duties. When this is all over, I'll have a word with Jeremy and David that all shit-shoveling duties will be split evenly between the three of them."

"They're not going to be happy about that, especially Jeremy."

Marcus shrugged. "Then they should have been born to a higher station."

Simon smirked. "And myself? I'm not nobility like you are. Should I be shoveling shit?"

Marcus stared at him, feigning dead seriousness. "Consider it done."

Enclos du Temple, Templar Fortress
Paris, Kingdom of France

Jeremy maintained a respectful distance as he followed Sir Matthew from his office. They entered the reception area and everyone present jumped to their feet when they spotted the leader of their order for the Kingdom. Sergeant Paumier rose from his desk and bowed deeply. "Sir Matthew, how may I be of assistance?"

"A man arrived here earlier in the day." He glanced over his shoulder at Jeremy. "About how long ago?"

"Within the past two hours."

"We need to identify him as quickly as possible."

"Of course, sir." Paumier hesitated. "We've had a large number of visitors, sir, and not all come through here. Is there anything that could help identify the man? Was he one of us?"

Matthew beckoned Jeremy to stand by his side and respond to the questions. Jeremy took several steps forward. "I'm not sure if he's a member of our order. He wasn't wearing our colors, however he was greeted at the gate by the guards on duty as if they knew him."

Paumier smiled slightly. "That helps, squire. I'll fetch the men who were on guard at that time, and bring them to you at once, Sir Matthew."

Matthew spun on his heel, heading back toward his office, leaving Jeremy uncertain as to what to do. Matthew glanced over his shoulder. "Stay with the sergeant. You may be able to help the guards remember the man. Once you find them, join me in my office."

"Yes, sir." Jeremy followed Paumier outside, confused when the man didn't head for the gate. "Shouldn't we be going to the gate, Sergeant?"

"No, the guard changed a quarter-hour ago. They'll be at the barracks now."

"Oh." He continued in silence, deciding second-guessing the experienced sergeant would only make him appear the fool and perhaps annoy the man. Time was of the essence. Marcus might have found the new location for the opium lounge already, and might be preparing to overwhelm what he was assuming were inexperienced civilians, instead perhaps facing an unknown number of Templars. And though Denys' personal guard looked quite fetching in their uniforms, he questioned how much experience they had against enemies who had spent years battling the Saracens in the Holy Land.

He suspected none.

They entered the barracks, Paumier barking at those inside. "Where are Sergeants Betyn and Tane?"

One of the men stood. "They just left, Sergeant."

"Didn't their shift just end?"

"Yes, Sergeant. They left immediately after."

"Did they say where they were going?"

"No, Sergeant. I believe they were assigned a patrol outside the walls."

Jeremy tensed. "How many left with them?"

The man's eyes darted at the lowly squire, then returned to the sergeant, the question going unanswered.

Paumier glared at the man. "Answer the squire's question, by order of Sir Matthew!"

The man snapped to attention. "There were at least ten of them."

"Can you name them?"

"I believe so. Most of them, at least."

Paumier gestured at the half-dressed man. "Make yourself presentable then report to Sir Matthew's office at once."

"Yes, Sergeant."

Jeremy followed Paumier out of the barracks and back toward the main building. "What do we do now?"

Paumier shook his head. "I'm not sure. What's this all about?"

Jeremy decided it wasn't his place to fill the man in on what was going on. "I'm afraid I cannot say."

Paumier frowned. "If a lowly squire can bring news that would have Sir Matthew in such a state, then I have no doubt whatever is going on cannot be good."

"You would be correct in your assessment."

Paumier bristled. "Then we must get to the bottom of this and find out where those men went."

De Montfort Estate
Paris, Kingdom of France

David arrived at Denys' estate and bypassed the main entrance, heading instead for where the personal guard should be marshaling. His tension eased slightly at the sight of the dozen men standing beside their horses, ready to depart. David came to a halt and hopped down from the horse, briskly walking toward Marshal Guillaume.

"I have a destination for us, Marshal. A house not far from here."

"How many are we facing?"

"An unknown number inside and four of the Prince's personal guard."

The man frowned. "They could pose a problem."

"Possibly, however our mission as explained to me by Sir Marcus is not to attack, but merely to intimidate them into releasing Thomas, and then determine who indeed is behind what is going on." He glanced about. "Is Sir Denys inside?"

Marshal Guillaume frowned, lowering his voice slightly. "I'm afraid Sir Denys hasn't returned from the Palace yet."

David's heart hammered as his eyes shot wide. "Is that normal? Could the Court still be meeting?"

Guillaume shrugged. "It has happened before, though it's rare. I have no doubt that many members of the Court are there, however after the official proceedings of the day, most return home to prepare for the parties in the evening. Few actually remain, as it is considered bad form to wear the same clothes in the evening as one did during the day."

David glanced down at the simple clothes he wore day in and day out, and in which he even slept. "Has word been sent to him?"

"Yes. After he didn't return, I had a messenger sent requesting instructions, as I knew you would be returning soon."

"When was this messenger sent?"

"Half an hour ago. He should have the message by now."

"Could he have forgotten?"

Guillaume vigorously shook his head. "Absolutely not. Sir Denys is a reliable man. I've never known him to shirk his duties, and I know he holds Sir Marcus in high esteem and would never intentionally let him down."

David suppressed a curse. "Then it must mean something has happened to him."

"That is what I fear as well."

David regarded him. "If you fear something has happened to him, would it be within your purview to proactively seek out the truth?"

Guillaume's eyes narrowed. "What do you mean?"

"I mean, shouldn't we be going to the Palace to find out what happened to your master?"

Guillaume drew a breath, his chest expanding, as if angered at himself for not having thought to take such action. "You're right." He mounted his horse, the others doing the same. "To the Palace!"

Palais de la Cité
Paris, Kingdom of France

Denys lay on the bed, his pain blissfully gone, the world swimming around him. Benuche sat in a comfortable chair in the corner, passed out. The small supply of opium he had brought had run out hours ago, and Denys was now coming down from the high clouds he still found himself engulfed within. There was a knock at the door and he mumbled permission for whomever it was to enter. The door opened and a messenger stepped inside, a folded paper on a tray.

"I have a message for you, Sir Denys."

Denys beckoned him over and took the page, everything a blur for a moment until his eyes focused. His heart rate picked up slightly, probably as much as it could in his compromised state, at the sight of his own family seal. It wasn't his personal seal, however it was the one his staff would use for household generated correspondence.

He snapped it and unfolded the page, finding a message from his marshal, and it was enough to have a surge of guilt rush through his body, giving him the energy to stand. "What time is it?"

The young man bowed. "I believe it is after eight, sir."

Denys cursed then stared at the opium pipe and bowl, the lamp still heating the nearly evaporated water, the vile substance once again having ruined his life.

You're so weak.

"Fetch my horse. I'll be leaving at once."

"Yes, sir."

The man left and Denys struggled to remain standing. Unsuccessfully. He dropped back down and drew several deep breaths, then closed his burning eyes as he steeled himself for what he must do. And as he did so, his world drifted away yet again, and he collapsed onto the bedding, swiftly lost in the peaceful bliss the opium brought him.

Enclos du Temple, Templar Fortress
Paris, Kingdom of France

Jeremy stood silently in Sir Matthew's office as their witness was grilled. The man had provided eight names, though was certain two others had left as well, whose names he didn't know.

"How can you not know men you've served with all these years?"

The man shook his head. "They're new, sir."

"The two you can't remember the names of?"

"No, sir, all of them."

Matthew's eyebrows shot up. "All of them?"

"Yes, sir, they're all part of a contingent that was transferred from Acre three months ago."

"I see." Matthew exchanged a quick glance with Jeremy who had already picked up on the implications. Templars were regularly rotated throughout Christendom, depending upon many factors, including age, health, and operational requirements. For a group to be transferred together all at once, wasn't common.

Sergeant Paumier cleared his throat. "Sir, I'm aware of who several of these men are, and if they're all like them, these are all healthy men, still able to battle should it be necessary."

Jeremy cringed at the thought of Marcus and Simon facing ten seasoned Templars on their own with nothing but Denys' personal guard to assist them.

Matthew eyed him. "You're telling me that ten healthy men were transferred from the front to here?"

"Yes, sir, assuming they're all as fit as the ones I'm aware of."

"Bring me their transfer orders."

"Yes, sir." Paumier left the room and Matthew turned to the witness.

"Are there any others that these men hang out with?"

"Well, we're all friends, sir."

"Yes, I mean were there any others transferred in with them that might not have left today?"

The man shifted uncomfortably.

"Speak! That's an order!"

The man stared at his boots. "Well, yes, sir, as a matter of fact, two of those that arrived at the same time are on guard duty right now."

"What post?"

"The main gate, sir."

Matthew exchanged a smile with Jeremy. "Have Sergeant Paumier bring them here immediately."

"Yes, sir."

Suspected New Opium Lounge
Paris, Kingdom of France

Simon stared down the road in both directions, holding a hand to his ear. "I don't hear anything."

"Nor do I," said Marcus. "There must be some delay."

"Would David not come here to inform us?"

"He would, unless he felt dealing with the delay was more important."

Simon frowned. "If those guards don't show up, we're in serious trouble."

"Yes, we are, though I'm sure Sir Denys will come through for us. He always has in the past."

"I hope you're right for Thomas' sake, but how long do we wait?"

Marcus sighed. "I fear we might not have much choice but to wait. With the Prince's guards here, it's not like the two of us can simply walk over there and intimidate them into laying down their arms."

Simon stared down the street at the men milling about behind the carriage. "I would be happy to try."

Marcus chuckled. "And I have no doubt you would succeed, however Templars would have then killed the personal guard to the brother of the King. That could spell disaster for our order."

Simon grunted. "Politics."

"It may be politics, but one doesn't challenge a king in his own kingdom. Even the Pope would be hard-pressed to defend us." Simon stamped his feet, the cold affecting them both. Marcus leaned closer to his horse, the beast's body heat substantial compared to his own. "Unfortunately, we're going to have to wait for either Sir Denys' men to arrive, or for the Prince to leave."

"I doubt there would be much serious opposition inside, certainly not opposition that has the experience we do."

Marcus agreed. "If only we knew for certain that Thomas was in there."

"What if I posed as a customer?"

Marcus regarded his sergeant for a moment, the idea intriguing, then shook his head. "It wouldn't work. One, you would have a hard time not inhaling at least some of the opium, making you useless in battle, but more importantly, there's no way you could know the operation had moved. I have little doubt they've only informed their most loyal of customers. You stumbling in unannounced would raise suspicions."

Simon frowned. "Like I said, I'll leave the thinking to you."

Marcus stared up at the moon, attempting to judge the time, determining once again it had been far too long since David had left. "Something is definitely wrong, and if it's beyond Sir Denys' control, then it can't be good."

"Could he have been delayed at court?"

"That's the only innocent reason I can think of. The rest are far less appealing."

"You think something might have happened to him?"

"Yes, I do, but what, I'm not certain. His only task was to determine if the Prince was there, and he accomplished that. However, perhaps somebody noticed his interest, or he went beyond his mandate and tried to find out where the new location was, raising suspicions."

"Do you think they would actually harm a member of the King's Court?"

"It's possible, especially if Templars are indeed involved, though I still find that impossible to believe."

"Why would you think it more possible if our order *was* involved?"

"Because they would want to keep their involvement a secret. We don't know how deep this goes, though with the Prince here, the use of this opium may be more widespread than simply Thomas' weak-willed neighbors. We already know an heir to the throne is involved, along with Sir Denys and several of his friends at the Court. The poor of the slums are of little importance to the Kingdom, but when those that administer it become affected, it could pose problems for all. It must be stopped."

"I agree."

Marcus stared into the dark, the streets still empty. "How we're going to accomplish that, I'm not certain. I just hope those men get here soon, so we can rescue Thomas. I fear if we don't find him by tonight, we'll never find him alive."

Unknown Location

Thomas sat in the cold corner of the basement that was now his dungeon. He had pulled himself out of the lake of pity in which he was drowning, and was once again puzzling a way out of the predicament in which he found himself. There had been a burst of activity on the other side of the wall just moments ago as someone had arrived. Part of him had wanted to shout for help, yet it would have been no use. All the voices had sounded cheerful, and had moved down the stairs and into the room on the other side of the wall that he had heard the preparations being made in earlier. It confirmed he was in their new location, and whoever had arrived must be an important customer to have been already notified. Raising the alarm would likely only get him killed that much quicker, though the arrival had confirmed one more thing.

There was a door at the top of the stairs.

If he could only remove his chain, he might escape to the outside, though what lay beyond the door, he didn't know, but anything had to be better than here. He grabbed at the chain around his ankle, straining with all of his might, yet it was fruitless. Even if he was at full strength, there was no way he was freeing himself of these irons, not without the key.

He stared at the chain disappearing under the door. The move here had been hasty, he had no doubt, and it was doubtful this chain had always been here. It meant it was likely added after the fact, at the same time he arrived, so how firmly it was attached at the other end was the question. He gently pulled on the chain, each rattle of its links causing him to cringe, and after several pulls, it became taut. He pulled harder, yet the chain didn't budge. He attempted several more tugs to no avail, then gently let the chain lie on the floor as he debated what to try next.

And a thought occurred to him.

He rose to his feet and stepped over to the door, feeding the chain through his legs. He pressed against the door then bent down at the knees and pulled the chain upward. The wood creaked in protest, then splintered, yet the door held. He relaxed his arms for a moment, regaining his breath, then tried again, yanking the chain taut, this time leaning backward, putting his entire body into the effort. More splintering was followed by a distinct crack, and the chain gave way slightly. He fell backward, but the chain held and he quickly regained his balance. He stepped over to the door and found it slightly ajar, the lock having been snapped.

He listened for any sign his success had been overheard, yet detected none. There was boisterous activity in the next room, though that was calming down, whoever had arrived likely settling in for their evening of opium use. He carefully opened the door and cringed at the creaking of a hinge. He froze, listening once again, and again it would seem no one was the wiser. He decided prolonging his situation would be unwise and instead yanked the door open enough for him to fit through. The hinges were so loud, he feared the dead would awaken with the sound.

The hall he found himself in was lit with several torches, allowing his eyes to follow the chain. The end was only paces away, attached to a large eyebolt screw twisted into a beam supporting the stairs leading to freedom. He bundled up the chain and brought it over to the hook, then grabbed the loop in both hands, twisting as hard as he could.

It refused to budge.

"I'll be right back," called someone, and Thomas' heart leaped into his throat. He rushed back toward his prison, letting out the chain as he did so, and cleared the door just as another opened at the far end of the hallway. He pressed the door closed and leaned against it, his chest heaving with fear, his pulse pounding in his ears as each gasped breath terrified him with the sound. Footfalls passed the door then went up the stairs, and he debated what to do. Should he make another attempt while the man was upstairs, or should he wait for him to return to the other room at the end of the hall?

The door upstairs opened then shut, making Thomas' decision for him. The man had left the building, and could be gone for some time. He hauled the door open, the creak of the hinges brief, then rushed back to the eyebolt. He gripped one side of the loop with two hands and put his body weight into it as he yanked it toward him. A loud chirp of metal scraping on wood was his reward, and renewed hope surged through him. He tugged once again, jerking at it, his full body poured into the effort, and once again, another chirp, and then it let loose. He repositioned and twisted the screw out of the wood, and moments later he was free.

Yet he wasn't free at all.

He stared at the steps and realized dragging the

chain would alert anyone to his escape. He began wrapping it between his opened hand and elbow as quietly as he could manage, yet he couldn't imagine no one had heard what he was doing. With none left on the floor, he took a tentative step up the stairs, wincing at the sound the old wood made with his weight.

He could see the door at the top, moonlight evident on the other side, indicating it indeed was the freedom he sought. He took another step, and another, then sprinted for the door. As he neared it, only paces away from freedom, it swung open, a startled man standing there, a man twice his size.

The man smiled. "Going somewhere?" A boot lashed out, hitting Thomas square in the stomach, sending him sailing down the stairs, tumbling head over heels before he landed painfully on the cold floor of the hallway he had just escaped. The man rushed down the stairs after him and grabbed him by the hair, hauling him into the room that was once again his dungeon. "I think you need to be taught a lesson."

He was kicked once again in the stomach and then again, the blows fierce and rapid. Thomas cried out, begging for the man to stop, yet the blows continued to rain down upon him.

The door was thrown open. "What the hell is going on in here?"

"I caught him trying to escape."

"Well, don't kill him yet. We have to wait for our friends to arrive. Tie him up, hands and feet, and stick a gag in him. Make sure it's tight. I don't want any more disturbances while the Prince is here."

"Yes, sir."

Thomas' eyes fluttered then shut as the world

around him went dark, and he realized he had no hope of surviving. If a prince of the Kingdom was involved, then these men had too much at risk to let a lowly denizen of the slums jeopardize their venture.

213

Palais de la Cité
Paris, Kingdom of France

David and the head of Denys' personal guard, Marshal Guillaume, marched up the steps to the Palais de la Cité then through the doors. A servant rushed over, surprised at the sight of a marshal and a filthy squire.

"You two cannot be here."

David didn't bother challenging the man, leaving that to Guillaume. "I am Guillaume, Marshal for Sir Denys de Montfort. It is urgent I see him at once."

The man said nothing, instead ushering them over to the side of the large entrance and out of the way of the nobility now taking notice of the unusual arrival. David glanced down at his chest, the red cross of his order, despite the lack of contrast with his brown tunic, still quite obvious to anyone who looked. He cursed himself for entering a den of wolves that despised his order. It had been a foolish oversight that he prayed didn't cost them everything.

"Sir Denys took ill earlier today," said the man.

"Is he all right?" asked Guillaume.

"He's…incapacitated, shall we say?"

David exchanged a glance with Guillaume, who was likely unaware what that meant, though David was quite certain Denys had given into the temptation of the opium once again.

"Where is he?" asked Guillaume.

"Follow me."

They were led down a series of corridors and finally

into a hallway lined with doors on either side. As they walked through, snoring could be heard beyond some, and behind others, squeals of delight as carnal pleasures were enjoyed. They stopped in front of one where there was nothing but silence. The man knocked and there was no answer.

"Is he inside this room?"

"He was the last time I checked."

Guillaume rapped on the door. "Sir Denys, it's Guillaume. May we enter?"

Again, there was no response.

David cursed and grabbed the handle, shoving the door aside, much to the shock of the palace servant. David and Guillaume rushed into the room, both gasping at the sight. An unknown man was passed out in a chair in the corner, an opium pipe gripped loosely in his fingers, attached to a bowl glowing from the heat of the lamp it sat over, the water inside long since evaporated. Denys was lying on a bed, passed out or worse, dead.

The servant rushed forward and put out the lamp then grabbed a pair of tongs from the nearby fireplace. He lifted the bowl and placed it on the hearth where it could safely cool. Guillaume stepped over to Denys' bedside.

"Sir, it's Guillaume. Can you hear me?"

There was a groan that at least let them know the man was still alive.

"Sir, you must wake up."

Another groan, this time louder, and Denys' head lolled from one side to the other. David cursed and stepped over to the bed, grabbing the man by the chin then slapping him on the cheek. "Sir, you must wake

215

up!"

Guillaume gasped in horror at David's actions, though he didn't stop him. David slapped Denys again, this time harder. "Sir, you must wake up!"

Yet it was no use, Denys' only response groans of protest and incomprehensible mutterings.

David turned to the servant. "You must have more experience with this than I. Is there anything that you can think of that we might be able to use to wake him?"

The man nodded. "This isn't the first time I've seen this sort of thing. I'll be right back." The man left, closing the door behind him, and the unknown man in the corner giggled uncontrollably before passing out once again. David stared at the near lifeless form of Denys, and realized there was no hope of the man giving the order they so desperately needed to send his personal guard to help Marcus and Simon.

His friends would be alone, facing an unknown number of opponents, and likely certain death.

Enclos du Temple, Templar Fortress
Paris, Kingdom of France

Jeremy stood in the corner as the two men were led into
Sir Matthew's office by Sergeant Paumier. They stood
at attention in front of Matthew's desk, staring directly
ahead, though it was obvious even to Jeremy that both
were nervous, though that could simply be fear from
having been called off the gate and led into the head of
the Order for the Kingdom with no explanation.

One of them reached up and wiped sweat from his
upper lip, then shifted his weight from one foot to the
other and back again. Jeremy wasn't an expert, but he
was quite certain this man was the more nervous of the
two, and Matthew picked up on the fact as well. He
pointed at the other one.

"You, wait outside until you're called for."

"Yes, sir." The man gave the other a look that
Jeremy could only interpret as one meant to tell him to
say nothing, then left the room. Paumier closed the
door and Matthew rose from behind his desk, stepping
around it and placing himself face-to-face with the man.

"Your name?"

"Sergeant Huchon."

"I'm going to give you the opportunity to tell me the
truth. If I find out you're lying, I will execute you
myself. Do you understand?"

The man gulped. "Yes, sir."

"I want to know what's going on."

"I don't know what you mean, sir."

217

"You know exactly what I mean. Sergeants Betyn and Tane left a short while ago with as many as eight other men, all off duty. I want to know why they left and where they went."

"I'm sure I don't know, sir."

"You just lied to me. Test me again."

The man trembled. "Honestly, sir, I don't know where they went. I wasn't told because I wouldn't be going with them. I had guard duty."

"But you do know *why* they went."

The man's head dropped into his chest, his shoulders slumping. "Yes, sir, I do."

"Tell me everything."

"I-I can't, sir. If I do, I'll be dead for sure."

"And as I've already informed you, if you don't tell me, I'll be killing you regardless."

"Yes, sir, however, you're a man of honor and will kill me mercifully. These men have no honor, and will make certain my death is slow and painful."

Matthew's demeanor suddenly changed, his clenched jaw relaxing, his piercing eyes softening. He put a hand on the man's shoulder. "Look at me."

The man raised his head.

"If you tell me what's going on, I will protect you. We will root out whatever vileness has penetrated these walls, and put an end to the danger you now face.

The man nodded. "Yes, sir. Thank you, sir."

"Now, why don't you tell me exactly what's going on."

A knock at the door had the man flinching. Sergeant Paumier opened it and was handed a sheaf of papers. "Is this all of them?"

"Yes, Sergeant."

The door was closed and Paumier quickly flipped through the pages before handing them to Matthew. "The transfer records for the men in question, sir, plus any others that came in at the same time."

Matthew took the pages, stopping at one. "It says here you came in from Acre."

"Yes, sir."

"In fact, all of these men came from Acre."

"Yes, sir."

"And you all were transferred at the same time?"

"Yes, sir."

Matthew scanned several more pages, then his eyes narrowed. He quickly flipped through the rest, staring at the same part of the page, then looked up. "You were all transferred here by Sir Gringoire de Melanes."

The man visibly tensed. "Umm, yes, sir."

"That's highly unusual. Do you have an explanation for it?"

The man shifted, clearly uncomfortable. "I suppose, sir."

"You suppose?"

"I mean, yes, sir."

"And what is your explanation?"

"All of us joined the Order at the same time that he did."

"Explain."

"We were all sergeants and squires of his household. When he joined the Order five years ago, we all joined with him."

"And now he arranged to have you all transferred here?"

219

"Not all of us, sir. About half of us."

"Why?"

"I'm not certain, sir."

Paumier put his hand on the hilt of his sword, the distinctive sound of several inches of the weapon unsheathing filling the room.

"That's the second time you've lied to me. Will you go for a third?"

"He wanted us here. We had no choice."

"Why did he want you here?"

The man stared at the floor. "To protect his shipments."

"What shipments?"

"If I tell you, sir, they'll kill me. They'll kill all of us."

"Not bloody likely," grumbled Paumier.

Matthew stepped closer to the man. "Is it opium?"

The man's eyes shot wide. "How did you know that?"

"Do you think I'm a fool? Why do you think you're here in front of me right now? Why is your friend outside this door? How do I have the records for all of your people already in my hand? I know everything. All I need to know is where was the operation moved to. Once I know that, then my business with you is finished, and you'll be taken into my custody for protection until this is over."

The man shook his head. "I wish I knew, sir. I would tell you without hesitation, for I am ashamed of what I've been forced to participate in."

"Would your friend know?"

"I think he may, sir. I saw him talking to Betyn before they left."

Matthew looked at Paumier. "Take him out the other door and put him somewhere secure with men we trust."

"Right away, sir." Paumier led the prisoner from the room, and Matthew turned to Jeremy.

"Bring the other one in, and have him leave his sword outside."

"Yes, sir." Jeremy stepped over to the door, praying that the man on the other side knew the location they needed, for the ten men who had left here minutes ago could have reached almost anywhere in the city by now.

And the lives of Marcus and Simon could already be at risk.

Suspected New Opium Lounge
Paris, Kingdom of France

Marcus cocked an ear. "Did you hear that?"

Simon nodded. "Yes."

"Did that sound like Thomas to you?"

"Absolutely. And it sounded as if someone were laying quite the beating on him."

Marcus cupped a hand to his ear. "I can't hear it anymore."

"Nor can I. That can only mean one of two things. Either they've stopped the beating—"

"Or he's dead," finished Marcus. He eyed the Prince's personal guard standing in front of the building, no longer milling about but staring at the structure, likely wondering about what they had just heard. He had no doubt he and Simon could handily best these likely inexperienced men, yet it would mean Templars killing the personal guard of the Prince, not to mention these men were doing nothing wrong.

They were innocent.

To kill four innocents to save one wasn't something he was willing to do just because the one was a friend. Reasoning with them was a definite possibility, though any element of surprise would then be lost, and those inside might simply kill Thomas before they could save him.

Where are Sir Denys' men?

He cursed. Something was definitely wrong. There was no way Denys would leave them like this, alone to fight an unknown number.

"What are we going to do?"

He sighed, regarding his sergeant. "I fear we have no options here. If Thomas is dead, then whether we make entry now or ten days from now is irrelevant. If his beating has stopped, then whatever prompted it is hopefully over and he'll be safe, at least for the next short while. As long as those guards are there, there's nothing we can do. If we attempt to fight our way in, even if we try to avoid the guards, they'll be prompted into action, because they'll believe we're after the Prince. I'm afraid unless we have numbers that force these men to lay down their arms peacefully, there's nothing we can do as long as they are here."

"And if Thomas is alive but dying from his wounds?"

"Then it is a burden I shall bear until the end of my days."

Palais de la Cité
Paris, Kingdom of France

"What's in that?" asked David.

The servant who had brought the noxious potion to aid Denys' recovery shook his head. "I'm not permitted to say, however it is used far too frequently within these walls."

David didn't pry any further. The Templars had their own rituals and potions that were known only to them, as he was certain most organizations did, including the King's Court. Everyone valued their secret elixirs they felt gave them an advantage over others, and their contents were closely held secrets.

And this one appeared genuine.

Denys was propped up in the bed now, sips of the potent brew forced into his mouth then his jaw clamped shut so the man would swallow it. And each time his Adam's apple bobbed, he came out of his stupor a little more. It didn't take long for his eyes to flutter open and for his head to jerk away from the hand gripping it.

He spat.

"What in the name of God is that?"

"You must drink it, sir, it will help you wake up," said Marshal Guillaume.

"No, let me go back to sleep," mumbled Denys.

David leaned closer. "Sir, it's David, squire to Sir Marcus de Rancourt. He needs you. We found where the Prince went. If your men don't arrive to help, he and Simon will surely die."

Denys stared up at him through foggy eyes. "Sir Marcus?"

"Yes. Remember, we're trying to find Thomas, we're trying to save him."

A flash of recognition had Denys sitting a little more upright. "Give me more of that."

The servant held the cup to Denys' lips. The nobleman took a sip then reached up and grabbed the cup, downing it in several large gulps, much to the consternation of the servant. He glanced over his shoulder at David.

"Well, he's going to be feeling that in a little while. That's enough to wake up a bear from its winter slumber."

"How long will it take?"

"With the amount he just took, he'll be bouncing off the walls in the next quarter-hour."

David looked at Guillaume. "I suggest we take him now and put him on his horse. By the time we get there, he'll be wide awake."

"I require the order."

David grabbed Denys by the chin. "Sir, I need you to order your men to assist Sir Marcus. Do they have your permission?"

"Yes," mumbled Denys. "Help them."

David glanced over his shoulder at Guillaume. "Satisfied?"

The man smiled broadly. "Absolutely."

Suspected New Opium Lounge
Paris, Kingdom of France

Thomas lay on the floor, agony racking his body. He was bound at the ankles now, his hands tied behind his back, a gag stuffed in his mouth, the chain now removed. Even if he had any strength left, there would be no point in struggling against the bonds, for the man who had caught him escaping stood in the hallway, keeping watch with the door open. There was no freeing himself now, and the man in charge had indicated once the Templars arrived, he would be dealt with.

His life would soon be over, and with how he felt at this very moment, he was glad of it.

His thoughts turned to Isabelle, and how once again she would be broken-hearted in her young life, though she was beautiful and would find someone else to move on with. And in time, she would forget all about him, and the feelings she once had, the plans they had made.

The very notion broke his heart.

"Your highness, I assure you, all is well."

"That's not what it sounded like to me."

Thomas perked at the angry tone.

"When I hear a man being beaten and screaming for help, it makes me wonder just what is going on here. I am a prince, an heir to the throne of the Kingdom of France. It was my understanding that you are honest men operating an honest business that valued discretion. Does that discretion involve beating men?"

226

"No, sir, of course it doesn't. We merely caught an intruder, and my man became overzealous. As soon as I discovered what was going on, I put an end to it, and the man we caught has been sent on his way, alive and well."

"If I find out you're lying to me, I will have the Court ban the use of opium, and put you out of business."

"I assure you, sir, that won't be necessary. If you would prefer, I can set you up privately so that you can enjoy our product in the comfort of your own residence."

"Do that. I won't be coming here again."

"Very well, sir."

The man guarding the door closed it as footfalls passed. Thomas cried out into his gag, but was too weak to make more than a groan that obviously went unheard as the unknown prince mounted the stairs and the door to the outside slammed shut, signaling an even worse fate for him.

For now that he had nearly cost his captors the business of one of the highest in society, he had no doubt the death he was about to face had just become all the more painful.

Enclos du Temple, Templar Fortress
Paris, Kingdom of France

Matthew stood in front of their second suspect, Sergeant Claren, his arms folded, his face grim. "You are one of Sir Gringoire's men, are you not?"

"I am, sir."

"How long have you served him?"

"Since I was a boy, sir. Almost thirty years."

"You are loyal to him?"

"Beyond question, sir."

"Yet your loyalty should lie with the Order."

"I believe I am capable of being loyal to both."

"Yet which would you choose first if the Order decided to punish your master? Against whom would you draw your sword?"

The man shifted, looking slightly away.

"Your hesitation gives me the answer I already knew I would get. You would betray the Order in a heartbeat, should it be necessary."

The man said nothing, instead returning his gaze upon Matthew.

"I know what's going on. Sir Gringoire had a group of you transferred here from the Holy Land in order to facilitate his smuggling operation."

Claren's eyes flared briefly, but he still said nothing.

"I know that a group of you left a short while ago. I need to know where they're going."

Again, the man said nothing.

"You've already been found out. I'm having word

sent to Jerusalem to have Sir Gringoire arrested. Your operation is finished."

The man smirked.

"You don't believe me?"

Claren stared directly into Matthew's eyes. "You have no clue what's going on here."

"Why don't you enlighten me?"

"I have no intention of betraying my master. I served him long before the Order, and I'll serve him long after. Do with me what you must, but you'll get nothing from me."

"Then perhaps I can offer you an incentive to cooperate."

"I find that highly unlikely."

"Those ten men that left here. Do you consider them friends?"

"I consider them my brothers."

"Then their lives are in your hands."

Claren eyed him. "What do you mean?"

"Those men that just left here have no idea that I've discovered your operation and their involvement. I may not know where they're going, but I know where they will eventually end up, and that is here. The moment they arrive, fifty of my men will surround them, arrest them, and then I will personally see to their executions. However, if you tell me where they went, I will send those same fifty men to arrest them before they carry out the orders I know they received, and they will survive to see another day." He jabbed a finger into Claren's chest. "But if they do carry out their orders, then it is too late for them. So, what's it going to be? You give me a location, and your brothers survive, as do you. Or you remain silent, and all of you die as well as any others that I discover are involved in betraying their vows and bringing dishonor upon this holy order."

The man's shoulders slumped, his chin dropping. "Very well."

David rode at the head of the column of soldiers, one hand on the reins, the other stretched out, gripping Denys by the arm. Marshal Guillaume was on the opposite side doing the same as they galloped through the nearly empty streets toward their destination. As each minute passed, Denys woke up a little more, then with a shocked gasp, the man inhaled deeply, his shoulders thrusting back, freeing himself of the two hands keeping him upright. He shook his head and took charge of the reins as the horse slowly eased up, no longer compelled forward by those on either side.

"All right, somebody tell me exactly what's going on."

David smiled. "It's good to see you back, sir, though I must warn you, the servant who provided you the potion indicated it will likely only last an hour at most before its effects wear off and you once again are incapacitated."

Denys cursed. "I've been foolish and selfish, and should I not survive the night, make certain Sir Marcus is aware that I am truly sorry I let him down. I pray we reach him in time." Denys turned to his marshal. "Should I fall either to the sword or my ailment, you are to follow Sir Marcus' or his sergeant's orders in this matter. Is that understood?"

Guillaume nodded firmly. "Absolutely, sir."

"Now, bring me up to date. What has been happening?"

David filled him in. "When we received your message that the Prince was at court, I had Jeremy bring it to Sir Marcus."

"He wasn't at the estate?"

"No, he and Simon left to investigate another matter. Sir Marcus and Simon returned, and the three of us went to the Palace and followed Prince Louis to his estate, then to a house on the outskirts of the slums where we believe Thomas is being held, or at least the men who took him are currently located. I immediately went to your estate and found that you weren't there. We were concerned for your safety, so we came to the Palace to seek you out and found you in an unfortunate state."

"Yes, unfortunate is one way of putting it. When this is over, I intend to be locked in my room until these cravings are finished. I can never again be compromised as I was today. Not only did I shirk my duties in court, but I've put lives at risk, lives that are precious to me. How far are we?"

"Not far, sir, though we should approach with caution. Unless we see or hear evidence of a fight, we should remain hidden. I will go ahead to where I know Sir Marcus and Simon are hiding, and inform them of our arrival."

"Very good. Let us pray we aren't too late due to my indiscretion."

Outside the Suspected New Opium Lounge
Paris, Kingdom of France

Marcus stared in stunned silence as the Prince emerged from the home and climbed into the rear of his carriage, the entourage departing and soon out of sight.

Simon grunted. "That was quicker than a teenager's first visit to a whorehouse."

Marcus glanced at his sergeant. "And you would know this how?"

"Not everyone I know was always a member of the Order."

"Uh-huh. Well, my understanding of this opium is that you enjoy it over a long period, like an evening of drinking. For him to leave so soon, he obviously heard what we heard, and wanted no part of it."

Simon spat. "I'm surprised as a member of that family, he didn't want to join in the beating."

Marcus agreed. "Perhaps he's not as vile as his brother, however his reasons for leaving aren't of importance. What is, is that the only visible guard on the house is now gone. I have no idea how many we may be facing inside, however I think this is the best opportunity we're going to have to save Thomas."

Simon gripped the hilt of his sword. "I agree. And should we find our brothers inside?"

"Then they are no brothers of ours, and my blade will show them no quarter should it become necessary."

Simon drew his sword. "Nor mine."

Marcus stepped from the shadows and crossed the

street, walking swiftly toward the house that lay ahead. As they approached the front step, he removed his plain black surcoat and tossed it aside, revealing his crisp white tunic with red cross, signifying he was a knight in the Templar Order. Simon did the same, revealing his black tunic with red cross, signifying his position as a sergeant.

They walked up a few steps to the door and Marcus paused, placing an ear against it. Hearing no evidence that their approach had been detected, he tried the door and it opened. He pushed it aside and crossed the threshold, his sword at the ready.

A hall was in front of him with several doors leading off to other rooms. He could hear voices arguing at the far end, someone clearly upset about the Prince's departure. A set of stairs led up to his left, another set down to his right. If the operation was set up as it was in the clothing shop, it was likely in the basement. The question was where would Thomas be held? He doubted he would be kept in the same room as the customers, and it was likely easier to keep him secure downstairs where there were no windows.

He indicated with a finger the stairs leading down and Simon nodded, taking the lead. He took a tentative step and the wood creaked under his feet. Marcus listened, and again there was no indication anyone had noticed. He motioned for Simon to proceed. His sergeant made it down the dozen steps and Marcus followed, both pausing at the bottom, still no sign anyone was aware of their presence.

Ahead of them was another hallway with several torches lit, held in sconces along the wall, revealing several more closed doors ahead of them. The first was just ahead on their right, and as Marcus approached, he noticed it was damaged.

He pushed the door aside, revealing a nearly pitch-black room. Simon grabbed one of the torches and held it out in front of them. Marcus gasped at the sight. Thomas was lying on the floor, bound and gagged and bloodied. They both rushed inside and Marcus pointed at the door. Simon closed it behind them as Marcus took a knee and drew his dagger, slicing through the bonds. He yanked the gag from the young man's mouth. Thomas struggled, his eyes squeezed shut, and opened his mouth to no doubt beg for mercy. Marcus clasped a hand over it.

"Thomas, it's me, Marcus. I'm here with Simon."

Thomas' eyes shot wide, then tears flowed as his entire body shook in relief. He reached up and grabbed Marcus, wrapping his arms around him as he sobbed. Marcus patted his friend on the back then gently pushed him away. "Can you walk?"

Thomas shook his head. "I don't know. They gave me quite the beating."

Marcus hauled him to his feet and held him out to see if he could maintain his balance. He let go and Thomas stumbled then regained his footing. He took several tentative steps toward the door. "I think I'll be all right. But if we have to run, just leave me."

"Not bloody likely," grumbled Simon as he handed the torch to Thomas. "Take this." Simon opened the door and peered in both directions, then indicated it was clear. Opening it all the way, he stepped into the hall, his sword at the ready, and Thomas followed him, stumbling once again. Marcus grabbed him and slung his arm over his shoulder as they headed for the stairway and freedom.

"Who the hell are you?"

Marcus spun toward the voice behind them and cursed. Simon charged forward, swinging his blade and silencing the man as Marcus carried Thomas up the stairs. The sound of chairs scraping on wood above them had him cursing. He held his sword out in front of him, rushing up the final few steps toward the door. Footfalls behind him, rushing down the hallway, indicated it was too late to make a stealthy escape. He booted open the door, the crisp air a false indicator of success. Swords clashed behind him but he ignored it as Simon would ask for help if he needed it, and a narrow hallway meant that even if he faced ten men, he would only be engaging one at a time.

And as he stepped through the door to make room for Simon, he gasped at the sight in front of him.

Ten Templars, all on horseback, were lined up on the street facing him.

It was over.

En Route to Suspected New Opium Lounge
Paris, Kingdom of France

Jeremy wasn't accustomed to being at the head of a column of fifty knights, and had to admit he enjoyed the feeling immensely as he rode beside Sir Matthew. After threatening all those involved with death, Matthew had quickly acquired the location, and they were headed there now in the darkened streets of a Paris night. He had little sense as to where they were, his experience in the city limited, all driven by landmarks usually viewed during the day. He knew how to get to the Templar Fortress from pretty much anywhere, as well as Thomas' home, the palace, Denys' estate, as well as Thibault's office. Everything else was in reference to those locations, though each time he was in the city, he became a little more aware of where things were.

The location had been described as on the outer edge of the slums, and having traveled to and from Denys' estate, he was well aware of where that edge was, and was quite certain they were almost there.

Matthew glanced at him, as if sensing his thoughts. "Don't worry, squire, we'll be there shortly."

Jeremy nodded. "I just pray we're not already too late. They're almost half an hour ahead of us."

"That may be, but they wouldn't have set our pace, otherwise they would have raised suspicions. I'm sure we've made up half that time."

Jeremy wasn't quite as confident, although said nothing, instead renewing his prayers that Matthew was

237

correct, and his friends were safe.

Approaching the Suspected New Opium Lounge
Paris, Kingdom of France

David indicated for the others to come to a halt, quite enjoying the position of de facto commander of a dozen men, though only Denys was a knight and a nobleman. "I'll go on ahead. They should be just around the corner."

Denys slumped forward in his saddle. David frowned at Guillaume. "I trust I can count on you and your men, despite his state?"

The marshal nodded firmly. "Absolutely. I have my orders."

"Thank you." David rode on ahead, cursing to himself at how things had gone so poorly today. They should have been here an hour ago, and Denys should have had his full faculties about him to command his troops.

Yet, here he was, a lowly squire, perhaps about to lead men that had no respect for him, into a battle against unknown odds. It was unacceptable, and he just prayed Marcus and Simon were where he left them, and nothing untoward had happened yet.

He rounded the bend in the road, nearing their hiding place, and spotted the house the Prince had stopped at.

And gasped.

The Prince's carriage was gone, along with the complication of facing down his guard. And with the interminable delay in Denys' personal guard arriving, would Marcus and Simon have waited? He had served with the men for over a decade, and was quite certain of what that answer was.

They would have taken advantage.

He made for the location they had been observing from, and found their horses tied up, but no sign of his friends. He cursed yet again, immediately beseeching the Lord for forgiveness.

What do I do now?

He stared at the house, debating what to do, when shouting erupted from inside. It could mean only one thing. Marcus and Simon had indeed attempted to rescue Thomas, and they had been discovered. The sound of scores of hooves pounding toward the scene had him staring down the road in the opposite direction from which he came.

And he smiled as he spotted almost a dozen men on horseback, their colors proudly on display, members of his order arriving to save the day. He could only conclude that somehow Jeremy had figured out where they were, and had convinced Matthew to assist. The Templars came to a stop in front of the house, lining up in a row of man and beast as the door flung open and Marcus stepped outside with a body over his shoulder, a body he assumed must be Thomas.

The shouts continued, and he heard the clash of swords, indicating Simon must be in a battle with others inside the house. He turned his horse to join his master when all of the knights drew their swords and pointed them at Marcus. David's jaw dropped as he realized these men weren't there to save the day, but instead must be the corrupt Templars referred to, the men who had broken their vows to their order and were profiting off the sinful opium.

He dismounted then turned the beast to face where Denys' men were waiting. He slapped the hindquarters, sending his ride galloping back to where the others were as he rushed silently forward, readying his bow and fitting an arrow.

Simon parried a thrust, knocking his opponent's sword to the side, then lunged forward with a dagger in his left hand, burying it deep in the man's throat. He dropped yet another body in the pile as the final man hesitated. Simon removed any additional hesitation by slicing the man's belly open with his sword. He listened for any other possible danger but heard nothing beyond the sounds of the dying at his feet, none having provided a challenge.

Just because a man has a sword doesn't mean he's a threat if he has no knowledge of how to use it.

He turned to see Marcus standing in the doorway, Thomas over his shoulder, and was surprised he hadn't already made his way to the horses.

"What's wrong?" asked Simon as he joined Marcus. Marcus stepped aside, giving him room to see what was amiss, and he cursed at the sight of ten of their brothers lined up on horseback, their swords drawn. "Well, I guess we have our answer."

Marcus agreed. "Indeed. It would appear our order is involved, and I'm disgusted by it."

"You'd be wise to hold your tongue, Sir Marcus. Our orders are to kill the three of you, though no one specified how quickly."

Marcus laid Thomas to the side so if this turned into a

fight, he could at least make a go of it. Simon stepped out onto the porch beside him, a sword in one hand, a dagger in the other, both dripping in blood, the silence behind him indicating the only foe they now faced lay ahead.

And what a foe.

There were no knights here, only sergeants and squires, though that meant little. Sergeants were experienced troops, sometimes even better fighters than the knights they served, and squires could be deadly as well, his own David and Jeremy second to none in battle. These would be formidable opponents even he and Simon would have no hope of defeating.

"I suggest you surrender and make things easier on yourself. For every one of us you kill, that's an extra day of torture before you die."

Simon grunted. "I count ten, and I have nothing planned for the next ten days, do you?"

Marcus shook his head. "No, I don't."

"So you intend to fight?" asked the man doing the talking.

"I do," said Marcus. He glanced at Simon. "And you?"

"Of course. Why would you think otherwise?"

"Well, I didn't want to speak for you since this is likely to the death."

Simon shrugged. "I'll take the five on the left, you take the five on the right?"

The men in front of them chuckled, which gave Marcus an indication of their overconfidence. These men assumed they would be victorious, therefore wouldn't take the initial attack as seriously as they should. It could give them the upper hand to remove two or three of them, perhaps even four or five, before the others realized they were at risk.

"Sounds good to me." Marcus readied his weapon, then took advantage of the first mistake their opponents had made. He charged forward, slicing his sword toward the man on the far right of the column, Simon doing the same to the left. None of the other eight men could engage as their horses were packed too tightly together. Marcus' initial blow was parried, then suddenly the man gasped in pain, tumbling from his saddle, an arrow embedded in his back.

Marcus ignored the question as to where the arrow had come from or who had shot it, and instead pressed the advantage of the confusion it had created. He swung his blade, slicing the throat of the second man as the others attempted to back up their horses so they could free themselves to join the fight.

Simon had made quick work of two at his end, and a third at his own end dropped from another arrow. The squires now had their bows ready, searching for a target, yet they clearly could find none in the dark.

Marcus smacked the side of one of the horses in his way and it bolted. He engaged the fourth on his side, but now everyone had found space and the man retreated, the remaining five still alive backing up to a safe distance. Two of the remaining squires aimed their arrows at them.

Marcus joined Simon for their final moments on God's creation. "It's been a privilege, Sergeant."

"The privilege has been mine."

Marcus raised his sword, clasping the hilt against his chest, the flat of the blade touching his nose and forehead as he closed his eyes and silently prayed.

Denys stared in confusion as David's horse raced toward them, riderless. His marshal indicated for one of the men to grab it, and he did so. "What do you think this means?" he asked, his mind a tumult of confusion.

"I think it means one of two things, sir. Either the squire is dead, or he sent this as a signal."

"Your recommendation?"

"These Templars are resilient. It would not surprise me if he were still alive and preparing to engage in battle."

"Sir, I hear something."

Denys glanced over his shoulder at one of the men.

"It sounds like swords, sir."

Denys cocked an ear but could hear nothing beyond the roar of his extreme fatigue. Guillaume listened for him.

"Definitely something going on ahead, sir, should we engage?"

Denys weakly tossed his finger toward the battle. "Engage."

His men surged around him, heading into the battle that lay ahead, a battle he couldn't join them in fighting. It was everything he could do just to maintain his balance. He leaned forward and hugged the neck of the beast beneath him, and prayed for the souls of those about to die.

Somebody roared a warning to their right and Marcus opened his eyes, turning his head to see David charging down the road. Another arrow loosed, bringing down one of the two archers that remained. The sergeants on their horses turned to engage, giving him and Simon a temporary reprieve.

"Run, David!" ordered Marcus as the three corrupt Templars closed in on the man on foot. David bolted to his right, evading the initial rush, and continued to sprint toward Marcus and Simon. Simon whipped his dagger, embedding it in the chest of the last remaining archer, eliminating any threat from a distance.

The three remaining hostiles turned toward them, and Marcus smiled at what was rounding the bend. He pointed behind their enemy and laughed. It had been his experience that when attempting to get an enemy to take his eyes off you in the heat of battle, it was far more effective to laugh than to shout.

And sure enough, one of them glanced over his shoulder, then eased up his charge.

A dozen men on horseback, Sir Denys' colors proudly on display, charged toward the scene, their swords drawn, and no matter how inexperienced they might be, there was no way the three remaining men would prevail, though he feared too many of Denys' men might still lose their lives.

"Let's finish this before anyone else dies."

Simon charged forward. "I assume they're excluded."

Marcus raised his sword. "You assume correctly."

David loosed his final arrow, embedding it in one of their enemy's shoulders, though not wounding him enough to take him out of the battle. He slung his bow and drew his sword as he followed his comrades into the fray. Marcus glanced over his shoulder at Thomas lying on the porch, and prayed that the boy survived, otherwise all of this would have been for nothing.

245

Marcus ducked, avoiding a swinging blade, then reached up and grabbed his opponent under his armpit, hooking his fingers under the chainmail. He yanked him from the saddle and tossed him onto the ground, then crushed his head with a single stomp of his boot. He grabbed the horse by the reins then swung onto its back, charging away several paces before pivoting to engage the remaining enemy. Simon was in the heat of battle with one of the men as Denys' guard descended upon the scene. Guillaume swung his sword, removing Marcus' opponent from the battle, the man not knowing what hit him.

And then there was one.

Denys' guard encircled him with their horses, their swords extended toward him, and Marcus rode up and penetrated the circle. He sheathed his sword, and Simon and David took up positions on either side of him. "Do you surrender?"

The man, his chest heaving with effort, shook his head. "The price of surrender is too high."

"The price if you don't is death."

"Death is preferable to some things, and it's definitely preferable to the future I can look forward to should I not die here tonight."

The pounding of hooves behind him had Marcus turning, then cursing at the sight of scores of Templars rounding the bend, all on horseback at a full gallop. His opponent smiled.

"How quickly the tide turns. How about you surrender?"

Marcus ignored the man, instead turning his horse around to face his new opponents.

"Sir Marcus!"

A smile spread as he recognized Jeremy's voice.

"Thank bloody God," said Simon. "I've never been happier to hear that little shit's voice in all my years."

Marcus chuckled. "Nor I."

Those at the lead of the column came to a halt in front of them, the remaining knights, all in their white surcoats with red crosses, surrounding everyone there, including Denys' guard. Marcus raised his hand in greeting to Sir Matthew Norris.

"Sir Matthew, it's a pleasure to see you once again."

"The feeling is mutual, Sir Marcus, however it would seem every time we do meet, something untoward has happened."

Marcus bowed slightly in his saddle. "Through no fault of my own, I assure you."

Matthew smiled. "Of course not."

Marcus indicated Denys' men. "These are the personal guard of Sir Denys de Montfort, and they are friends."

Guillaume sheathed his sword and his men followed suit, the rest of the Templars visibly relaxing. Matthew nudged his horse forward, staring at the one remaining hostile.

"And your name is?"

The man's shoulders slumped. "Sergeant Hew."

"He's on the list, sir," said Jeremy.

"Yes, indeed he is."

"What list?" asked the man.

"The list of you and your brothers, everyone who's involved, all loyal to Sir Gringoire de Melanes. Your operation is finished."

The man grunted. "I highly doubt that."

247

"Word has already been sent to the Holy Land to have your master arrested, as well as all others who had previously sworn allegiance to him before joining the Order."

The man laughed. "You'll never find him."

"I think you're mistaken." Matthew waved a hand at several of his men. "Arrest him."

A growl erupted from the man, turning into a roar as he raised his sword and urged his horse forward. Marcus repositioned to protect Sir Matthew and raised his sword to parry any thrust when an arrow embedded itself in the man's chest, along with a dagger, ending the final charge of Sergeant Hew.

Matthew sighed. "I was hoping to interrogate him. We'll have to rely on those we have in custody at the Fortress."

"Is that all of them?" asked Marcus.

"Except for their master and perhaps some still in the Holy Land. When the message arrives in several weeks, they'll take him into custody and put an end to this entire affair." Matthew glanced over his shoulder at David and Jeremy, tending to Thomas. "Is that young Thomas Durant?"

"It is."

"I hope he's worth it."

"He is to me, sir, and in rescuing him, we've put an end to a stain on our order's reputation."

"This is true. Are there any inside?"

"I believe Simon removed them from God's creation, however it should be swept."

Matthew gave the order and a dozen men dismounted and searched the premises, the lead man

248

coming outside a few minutes later, shaking his head. "Nothing but bodies, sir."

"Then it would appear our business here is done. It's not the way I like to end a night, not in a city such as this, though it is satisfying to have done some good." He turned to one of his men. "Bring the carts forward."

The man rode off, and a few moments later, a group of squires and sergeants arrived with carts. The bodies of the disgraced Templars were piled in the carts, then a search inside was swiftly completed, nothing found that could tie the night's events to the Order. Within minutes, the column was returning to the Fortress, and David and Jeremy had left for Denys' estate in a cart with Thomas in the back.

Matthew turned to Marcus. "Will you be joining us?"

"I will tend to Thomas first by bringing him to Sir Denys' estate. I will report to you in the morning."

"First thing, Sir Marcus, first thing."

"Absolutely, sir."

Matthew turned and rode away.

"Do you think this is the end of it?" asked Simon as they rode to join Denys and his men, the incapacitated nobleman, passed out in his saddle, retrieved by his men the moment the battle had finished.

Marcus shook his head. "I'm not so sure. There's something Hew said that has me concerned."

"What?"

"He said, 'You'll never find him.'"

"Yes, I was wondering about that. It's an odd thing to say if his master is manning his post in the Holy Land. There's no way he could know what's happened here before our forces could be notified to arrest him. What do you think it means?"

"I think it means Sir Gringoire isn't in the Holy Land, and hasn't been for some time."

Simon cursed, staring at Marcus. "You know where he is, don't you?"

Marcus nodded. "I think I know exactly where he is, or at least where he will be."

The Slums of Paris, Kingdom of France

David and Jeremy were positioned on the rooftops as spotters and backup should things go wrong. Marcus and Simon, as well as Sir Matthew and half a dozen of his men, were secreted in an alleyway. One of their prisoners, arrested at the Fortress, was held tightly by two sergeants, his hands and feet in chains affording no hope of escape, his mouth gagged so no warning could be shouted.

Nothing was left to chance.

David executed a birdcall from above.

Simon drew his sword. "This is it."

Marcus held out a steadying hand. "Let's wait until he gets off his horse."

The second birdcall was the final signal and Marcus charged from the alleyway, sword drawn, followed by the others. They rushed across the street toward the clothing shop, their target still mounting the steps, his key extended in front of him.

"Stay where you are!" ordered Marcus as the men made a half-moon around the front of the shop. The man turned, his arm slowly rising, fear on his face as his hands shook.

"What's going on here? Why are you accosting me in such a manner?"

"I think you know why," said Marcus. "It's over."

"What's over?"

"We know who you are."

The man eyed him. "Of course you do. We met

yesterday in my shop. Oh, that renter came by here. Is that why you're here?"

"You can stop playing us for fools, Sir Gringoire. Like I said, we know who you are."

The man's eyes narrowed. "Sir Gringoire? I don't know who that is."

"I know that to be a lie."

The man lowered his arms slightly. "I have no idea what you're talking about, but you have no authority over me. If you wish to have me arrested, then make it members of the King's guard, not Templars whose authority comes from Rome and not Paris."

Matthew stepped forward. "When it involves a deserter and a traitor to our order, our authority extends to the four corners of the world." He gestured over his shoulder toward the men still standing in the alleyway they had been hiding in. Their prisoner was hauled forward and shoved to his knees in front of the shop. Simon reached over and yanked the gag from the man's mouth.

Marcus pointed at the shopkeeper. "Is this your master?"

The man nodded.

"And his name is?"

"Sir Gringoire de Melanes."

The shopkeeper stared down at the man, shaking his head. "I don't know who this is, but I've never met him before. I'm not going to stand here and be accused of being someone I'm not. I cooperated with you yesterday, and that's the end of my involvement."

Marcus tapped the prisoner with his boot. "Tell us what you told us earlier, how you could prove it was him."

"He has his family's crest tattooed on his left shoulder, and the cross of our order on his right."

Simon swiftly strode forward and reached out with both hands, tearing the man's sleeves off before he could defend himself, revealing the two tattoos. Simon smiled, turning toward Marcus. "If that's not proof, I don't know what is."

Gringoire glared at the prisoner. "You fool! I should have known it would be you who couldn't keep his mouth shut!"

Matthew swung a finger toward Gringoire. "Take him to the Fortress. I'll deal with him later." His men sprang into action, grabbing the now silent Gringoire, and soon all that remained were Marcus and his men, along with Matthew. He turned to Marcus. "How did you know?"

Marcus regarded him. "You mean besides the fact he had tattoos that matched what your witness said?"

"Yes, besides that."

Simon eyed Marcus. "You knew last night before you ever heard of the tattoos. You said you knew where he'd be. Explain yourself, otherwise I'll accuse you of witchcraft."

Marcus chuckled. "Actually, we were both suspicious. If you recall, when we visited the shop yesterday, we both had our suspicions as to whether he was telling the truth. I suspected he was lying, however he did play his part well. I tested him by having you show him the cushion with Prince Louis' coat of arms on it. Remember, he said he didn't recognize it. At the time, I couldn't be sure if he was telling the truth, however if he did recognize it as the coat of arms of one of the men who frequented his opium lounge, I

253

would have expected at least a reaction out of him, though there was none.

"This suggested several possibilities. One was that he truly was innocent, and had no idea what was going on in the basement of his shop. Another was that he was an exceptional liar. And yet another, was that he may be involved, but didn't participate in the day-to-day operations."

"Would that make sense? Why wouldn't he participate?" asked Matthew.

"Remember, it was a night-time operation, and this man works all day in his shop. So, if he were involved, it would be quite the thing for him to work such long hours day in and day out."

"That still doesn't explain to me how you knew."

Marcus regarded his sergeant. "Do you remember that both Sir Denys and Mrs. Thibault immediately recognized the coat of arms, and do you remember what she said when we first showed the cushion to her?"

Simon shrugged. "I don't remember if I even had breakfast this morning. What did she say?"

"She said, of course she recognized it, and that anyone who lives in Paris knows it, and knows to keep clear."

Simon's head bobbed slowly as he recalled the conversation. "Yes, I remember her saying that. But again, how did that make you suspect the shopkeeper?"

"Because of something else he said. He said that his brother had gone to the Holy Land and come back broke with all these wares to sell. That meant they are from Paris. He also said that he had a friend connected to the nobility and the affairs of the heart that he could sell these sheer fabrics to. It just didn't ring true. He would have us believe that a man who's lived in Paris for perhaps his entire life, and has connections to the nobility, doesn't recognize the coat of arms of Prince Louis, an heir to the throne of the kingdom and city in which he lives?"

Simon's jaw dropped. "I hadn't thought of that."

Marcus turned to Matthew. "When Jeremy told me that Sir Gringoire is actually from Reims, it convinced me that the shopkeeper and Sir Gringoire were actually the same person. A man who lives his life in Reims would be expected to know the coat of arms of his king, but not of his king's brother. In Paris, everyone knows it because Prince Louis is notorious for running down pedestrians and kidnapping young women for his own carnal pleasures. If the shopkeeper had indeed been raised in Paris, he would know this, and would have reacted when he was shown the coat of arms. Because he didn't react, and denied recognizing it, it meant either he was lying, or he wasn't from Paris at all, which meant he was lying about how he had started the shop. Then there was the matter of the renter."

Simon held up a finger. "Yes, if there was anybody who I suspected was Sir Gringoire, it would have been him, wouldn't it? I mean, he's the one paying the rent."

Marcus shook his head. "No, we now know that he wasn't paying the rent at all. What's more likely, is that at the end of business each day, this so-called renter would come to the shop to receive instructions from Gringoire and update him on any situations that may have arisen the night before. Remember, if Gringoire had been there when Thomas was kidnapped, Thomas would have been dead immediately. Instead, they waited for instructions. Also, as Thomas has since told us after we freed him, the man had said that they were waiting for Templars to arrive, who would be executing him. That to me meant not only were there no Templars actually in the opium lounge while it was operating, the shopkeeper, Gringoire, was the one giving the orders. I believe the man who ran the opium lounge for Gringoire came here last night at the close of business, told him what had transpired the night before with Thomas, then was given instructions to relay to his men at the Fortress."

"Why wouldn't he just tell them himself? They're his men, after all."

Marcus shook his head. "He couldn't. Remember, he could never be seen at the Fortress in case he was recognized. He was supposed to be stationed in the Holy Land. The instructions were relayed by the so-called renter, and Gringoire's men immediately left in order to execute them."

"But why did he do it?" asked Sir Matthew. "Why betray the Order, why betray his vows?"

Marcus shrugged. "You'll have to ask him that, though I suspect with him only being a member of the Order for five years, and this being a well-executed plan, I think he's been planning this for years, perhaps before he even joined the Order. Perhaps he arrived there with good intentions, and as we know, not all men are cut out to be a Templar. Some go into our order for the glory, however quickly tire of the constant prayer, the celibacy, and the pious life. If he was a nobleman used to enjoying the indulgences available to someone of wealth, he may have realized the Order wasn't for him."

"Then why not just leave?" asked Simon. "It's not prison."

"You're forgetting, he would have handed over all of his worldly goods to the Order, so would have nothing if he left it."

Matthew scratched his chin, his head slowly bobbing. "So, rather than leaving the Order officially, he set up this smuggling operation to bring opium from the Holy Land and into Christendom, so he could restore the wealth he had given up."

"Exactly. He transferred a contingent of his men who were loyal to him here, and he likely has a group still there so that he can continue to funnel everything through."

"But why come here? Why not stay and make sure things ran smoothly?"

"Because if he did, he'd be forced to continue to live the life that he despised. In order to escape the life of a monk, he deserted and came here, setting himself up as a shopkeeper. Word would have eventually arrived in Paris of his abandonment of his post, though I'm guessing he probably set things up so that it would appear he was taken by the Saracens on patrol, so no one would look for him because they assumed he was dead."

Matthew shook his head in amazement. "I realize much of what you just said is conjecture, however it all makes sense, and I suspect when all is found out, most if not all of it will prove true. We'll hopefully know in the next several weeks if your theory about his desertion is correct, as I'm sure an official report is already on its way." He extended a hand to Marcus and he took it, shaking it firmly. "You've done well once again, Sir Marcus. I am in your debt, should you ever need anything."

Marcus bowed. "I was merely doing my duty to the Order and my friend. No debt exists between us."

Matthew shook Simon's hand as well, then David and Jeremy's. He wagged a finger at Jeremy. "Your squire did well yesterday. He showed initiative that saved a lot of lives, and saved the Order from embarrassment or worse. If I do not owe you, Sir Marcus, perhaps you would allow me to reward your squire."

Marcus smiled. "Of course, sir."

Matthew looked at Jeremy. "Is there anything that I can do for you?"

Jeremy shifted nervously, unaccustomed to being addressed by such a senior knight in such a manner. "Well, maybe you could order David to shovel all the shit instead of me?"

Matthew tossed his head back and roared in laughter, the others joining in, all except for David, who stood wide-eyed, his mouth agape, horrified that the head of the Order for the entire Kingdom might just grant Jeremy his wish.

Matthew slapped Jeremy on the back. "While I do owe you a debt of gratitude, I cannot punish poor David here. However, from this day forward, the shit shoveling duties will be divided equally between the two of you. How does that sound?"

Jeremy grinned. "Like Heaven, sir. Like Heaven."

En route to Durant Residence
Paris, Kingdom of France

Thomas rode with Isabelle at his side, Marcus and Simon ahead of them, the squires behind. Thibault and Enzo had left earlier in the morning once word had arrived that the ringleader behind his kidnapping was under arrest, and most of the corrupt Templars were dead. Denys had remained at his estate under lockdown, as he struggled to recover from the severe dependency he had developed. A doctor from the King's Court had assured everyone that Denys would be fine in time, and also revealed that he was treating several others with the same affliction, including Benuche. Thomas himself wasn't fairing too poorly, his exposure limited. While he had felt its effects, and they had indeed been quite pleasurable at first, he had quickly developed a dislike for it and had stopped himself from inhaling whenever he wasn't watched.

As they approached his neighborhood, the landmarks growing more familiar, he again questioned why they were returning to his home. He had heard it was burned in a fire, and had no desire to see the only home he had ever known destroyed. As they rounded the final bend, his home visible just ahead, he gasped at the sight of scores of his neighbors gathered out front of a newly built façade, his home looking better than it ever had.

Cheers erupted along with the sound of scores of hands clapping, and his chest ached at the outpouring of love from those he had assumed hated him. Tears flowed down his cheeks as they slowed, and he glanced over at Isabelle, a smile spread across her face, her own tears gushing.

Marcus brought the entourage to a halt, and they all dismounted. Thomas was surrounded by his neighbors, hugs and back-slaps delivered, cheeks kissed, all leaving him overwhelmed. Chapon and his family pushed through the crowd, carrying baskets of baked goods, giving him an explanation as to why they had departed early.

Marcus held out a hand and beckoned Richart forward, a man he had known all his life. "You can thank Mr. Richart for helping rebuild your house. He and his son coordinated everything, and along with your neighbors, they repaired all the damage."

Thomas shook his head in disbelief. "I don't know what to say. All I can say is, thank you. Thank you from the bottom of my heart." His chest heaved. "And know that I believe my mother and father are looking down upon us from Heaven, and sending their thanks as well." He held out his hand for Isabelle and she took it. "We intend to make this our home during the winter months. I had my doubts as to whether we would be happy here, but what you've shown me today, tells me that we made the right decision. Not only will I be starting my family here, but Isabelle and our future children can live here knowing they are never alone, and that they will always be surrounded by you, my extended family, and the love we all share for each other as neighbors." He bowed deeply, and tears erupted once again as he was embraced.

"Don't forget the part I played!" shouted someone from behind the wall of flesh enveloping him. The crowd parted and Thibault stepped through with Enzo. "After all, I am the one who foot the bill."

His eyes bulged. "You did?"

"Do you think all that wood is free?"

He extended a hand. "Thank you. I don't know how I can ever repay you."

Thibault winked. "I'll figure out a way, I assure you."

Nervous laughter sprinkled through the crowd and Chapon began handing out food to break the tension. Several other shopkeepers from the neighborhood left and quickly returned with their own wares, and a street party such as the neighborhood had never seen was soon in full swing.

Thomas and Isabelle stepped away from the crowd and joined the Templars on the newly reconstructed front porch of his home, Thibault and Enzo following them.

"So, you're going to make an honest woman of Isabelle?" asked Thibault.

Isabelle stared up at Thomas, as happy as he had ever seen her. "He hasn't asked me yet."

Thomas' eyes bulged. "Wait a minute!" He rushed inside, ignoring the repairs and the freshly scrubbed surfaces, and ran up the stairs to what had once been his parents' bedroom, left untouched since the death of his father. He pulled open a drawer and rummaged through it, finally finding what he was searching for. He ran back down the stairs and out into the sunlight, his chest heaving.

He drew a deep breath as he stood in front of Isabelle, then dropped to one knee, holding out the ring that had once belonged to his mother. "Isabelle

Leblanc, will you marry me?"

Simon leaned closer to Marcus. "I guess we don't have to tear his balls off."

THE END

ACKNOWLEDGMENTS

This novel was written during the beginning of the COVID-19 pandemic, and while the Black Scourge might have been confused with the Black Death, I intentionally avoided any negative parallels. While the pandemic will end in time, as did the Black Death, the scourge referred to in this novel likely never will.

One theme that did unintentionally develop, was that of neighbors helping neighbors. Thomas had thought his neighbors had turned against him because of his newfound success, and when he needed them most, they came through for him, just as we see all around us in these dark days.

Neighbors helping neighbors.

I redrafted these acknowledgments many times, and finally gave up, cutting the commentary with respect to the selfish who would ignore the rules while the vast majority stayed at home to fight this virus, and perhaps even this brief paragraph is what I had intended to eliminate. All I will say is this:

Now is not the time for panic, politics, or protest.

Now is the time to be a good neighbor, for when life returns to normal, rest assured, it will be as vile as it always was, and those agitating now will be in their element once again.

As usual, there are people to thank. My dad, as always, for the research, and Deborah Wilson for some horse info, and of course, my wife, daughter, my late mother who will always be an angel on my shoulder as I write, as well as my friends for their continued support, and my fantastic proofreading team!

To those who have not already done so, please visit my website at www.jrobertkennedy.com, then sign up for the Insider's Club to be notified of new book releases. Your email address will never be shared or sold.

Thank you once again for reading.

CPSIA information can be obtained
at www.ICGtesting.com
Printed in the USA
LVHW031941300721
694139LV00005B/394